W9-CHC-044

In the Hold

In the Hold

Vladimir Arsenijević

Translated from the Serbo-Croatian
by Celia Hawkesworth

ALFRED A. KNOPF NEW YORK

1996

THIS IS A BORZOI BOOK

PUBLISHED BY ALFRED A. KNOPF, INC.

Copyright © 1996 by Celia Hawkesworth

All rights reserved under International and Pan-American Copyright Conventions.

Published in the United States by Alfred A. Knopf, Inc., New York, and simultaneously in Canada by Random House of Canada Limited, Toronto.

Distributed by Random House, Inc., New York.

http://www.randomhouse.com/

Originally published in Yugoslavia as *U potpalublju* by Vreme Knjige, Belgrade, in 1995.

Copyright © 1995 by Vreme Knjige

Library of Congress Cataloging-in-Publication Data

Arsenijević, Vladimir, [date]

[U potpalublju. English]

In the hold : a novel / by Vladimir Arsenijević.

p. cm.

ISBN 0-679-44657-5 (alk. paper)

I. Title.

PG1619.1.R74U1713 1996

891.8′235—dc20 96-25550 CIP

Manufactured in the United States of America

First American Edition

For Sladjana and Filip

In the Hold

PART I

October 1991

About Bedtime Dilemmas—Angela and Me and Someone Else (Whose Appearance Is Awaited)—Lazar's Visit—A Sketch About Executors and Commanders—Why Angela's Courage Scares Me—Voices from the Torrent

About Bedtime Dilemmas

At a given moment, which I now fail to recall, somewhere between the twenty-fifth and thirtieth year of my life, I conceived the need for a special daily ritual. This ritual comes under the category of domestic habits that, when we are teenagers, help us to hate our fathers in precise detail. In their middle age, fathers cling frantically to such habits and seem to us sadly reconciled to the delusion that life is merely a list of well-worn actions that are never questioned. My own first mature ritual consisted of the following: every afternoon, after work and lunch, I would withdraw to the bedroom of Angela's and my flat in Molerova Street, where I abandoned myself to a kind of nightmare half-sleep. Sprawled on my back on the double bed, respecting the unwritten canon of Habit, I lay completely motionless. My eyes closed, my lids did not betray me with so much as a flicker. But I was not asleep. Curled up inside my self, I was simply tormenting myself, enacting for a nonexistent audience the idyll of a postprandial sleeper; deep in myself, perfectly wide-awake, I was in fact disintegrating in indecisiveness.

Although I never did manage to understand this kind of negative transcendental meditation, I practiced it at length, and systematically. It would certainly have been more honest, and probably healthier, to take an actual nap. My father's conscience was always impeccable: he would snore alarmingly, every afternoon, without regard to the revulsion that I endeavored to transmit from my own room, hoping, in a fifteen-year-old's pathetic delirium, that he might simply fall apart, in his sleep, under the pressure of the hatred I was directing toward him. And now, wedged in the gap between Weariness and Guilt, I was not even capable of falling asleep properly. I closed my eyes, but behind that curtain I was quite conscious. At those moments (when, from the outside, I appeared calm, having abandoned myself to revitalizing sleep), my unease was so great that my face ached from an inner spasm, and if I had wished, for the sake of experiment, to arrange my lips into a smile, it would have meant traveling half the world, from one cheek to the other.

If I remember rightly, the October evenings of 1991 were sort of flaky, and greenish yellow. For days a strange cloud floated over Molerova Street, I'm certain of that at least. A swirling wind scattered crushed leaves below the window of the four-story yellow brick building. When the evenings are as mangy as this, and when the air smells of the darkness of approaching autumn, even an amateur afternoon sleeper doesn't feel like getting up. Any activity holds the possibility of trouble, so he is afraid of washing his hair because the shampoo is bound to sting his eyes, he shrinks at the thought of the headache in store for him after he has used the hair dryer, he is fearful, also, of the bad sleep he knows will exhaust him, and if he picks up the telephone to call someone he's fond of, he shouldn't be surprised if the simple machine overwhelms him, or if (ignoring his halt-ingly expressed need for mutual contact without intimacy) the friendly voice at the other end of the line coldly refuses his request for verbal prostitution—as a kindness to him, without agreeing to a price—and instead wrings him out to the point of senselessness.

At that time, as far as the art of afternoon dozing was concerned, I had already progressed well beyond the amateur, but then again I trembled, overcome by that spe-cial sleeper's confusion. I knew, of course, that none of the above could be particularly terrible in itself, but I lacked the energy to confront everyday life. Troubles attract troubles, I reflected, they will leapfrog over one another, and I shall not be able to withstand that torrent when it starts to roar. I saw myself, calm in the face of the impending catastrophe, like a calf blinking meekly before the sentence of the butch-er's hammer.

So even if Angela called from the living room, I

repeated to myself, I would let her shout; no matter what it was, I wouldn't respond. Her voice, *via hysteria*, would induce a certain degree of calm. It would vibrate through the springs of the bed, but I would resist it, my eyes shut tight. The need to experience fully a guilt that eluded definition—guilt because of my own body, which determined me so clumsily—would undoubtedly be stronger even than that voice. Because then, as always before, and afterward for that matter, I could never agree with the choice of toes that had been allotted me, with the size of my shoes, my height, weight, the dimensions of my head, the color of my eyes, my sex, and all the other data on my health record card, and it seemed silly to say the least that I should have to accept that body as *mine*, when, despite all, I floated inside it, like an embryo in amniotic fluid.

By contrast with the bodily shell that I had never been able to understand, the sweatshirt in which I was lying that October exuded the brilliant essence of Sweatshirt. As far as I could recall, it had never met me with surprises, every day it retained the qualities it had had the previous day: made precisely to appeal to me, I had bought it to do myself a favor, it wasn't cheap, but that kind of favor is beyond price. And when, one day, I came to throw it away, I knew (and this is the kind of thing I concerned myself with as I slept/didn't sleep) it would be as though I had thrown away an irreplaceable version of myself: a large full stop at the end of an uneven chapter.

Angela and Me and Someone Else (Whose Appearance Is Awaited)

Angela did not come to wake me until just before dinner, waddling in with her immense stomach. In her advanced pregnancy, she complained often of gas and cystitis. She was capable of peeing three times in the course of a single hour. I sat on the edge of the bath waiting for my turn, while she, her legs apart, beat a drumroll, with her undirected golden jet, on the enamel toilet bowl. Then, with a professional movement of her hand, she felt her thighs, swollen with excess water. And only when she had stood up and, in one stroke, despite her protruding stomach, pulled up her panties, which had slipped down to her knees, did she say, as though there were some connection: "Rome!" The whole of Angela's face, at that moment, glowed with badly focused reproach. Perhaps I was supposed to be surprised, but I had already had a similar experience. A year earlier, in the middle of Rome, when we were winding up the second week of our honeymoon, laden with postcards and stamps that she had ruined by pouring a cup of hot chocolate over them, with an identical expression of reproach, she had pronounced a strikingly similar word, as though it were a triumphant formula. Then, she had said: "London!"

After that, we roamed through the city, arm in arm. I am sure that if she had wanted to see them, there were many things for Angela to discover: monasteries surrounded by heavenly gardens filled with lush palms and orange trees, scattered over the little hills from which one could see the whole center of the ancient city; conglomerations of ruins reflecting the passing centuries; blackened flights of steps where one's footsteps rang out chillingly; narrow, damp streets; huge complexes of villas with courtyards full of cypresses and pine trees; the infernal September heat; the vaults of sixteen hundred churches, Renaissance cupolas glinting in the morning sun; the terraces of luxury attic flats overgrown with ivy, where dark-skinned men stretched out to sun themselves; lanes in which all one could buy was equipment for church services (miters and all that incredible clothing); stone angels with drawn sabers; modern concubines on motorbikes; obelisks on top of elephants; and, finally, the Catacombs, little chapels decorated with the crushed bones of Capucin monks. But Angela was indifferent to it all, even after our honeymoon, or else she was secretly disappointed. The only thing that had really enchanted her in Rome was a bookshop, a dingy little place with an unwholesome smell, where she unearthed an ancient *London Streetfinder*, with a supplement of touched-up photographs of famous sights, and she caressed it for hours with an adoring gaze.

Pronouncing "Rome" defiantly and with special meaning, she turned on the tap. As well as soaking two pieces of paper, the jet washed away my sleeper's bad temper. Pharaoh, the cat Angela had brought into our shared life as an integral part of her dowry, wound himself around my legs. I gave him a secret kick (Angela would have been furious) and followed my wife in the manner of a faithful animal, the way Pharaoh follows me when he's hungry, along the complicated journey through the hall and dining room into the kitchen. It was not until we got there, and she had put on the water for tea, that Angela decided to pursue the subject broached in the bathroom. "I've been thinking," she said, looping up her hair. "We really had a great time in Rome, didn't we? We don't need to go to New York at all. The two of us and the baby could live very nicely in Rome! And it's closer, you know!" Belgrade was, quite simply, exhausting her. That morning on the No. 7 tram, going to visit her parents and her doctor in New Belgrade, she had been obliged to avert her eyes from her dreadful fellow passengers. Naturally, she did not want to look out the window, in order to avoid confronting the Tehranesque panoramas, so she turned her attention to the book I had recommended to her as City Transport Services reading matter. Maybe I ought to have given it more thought, but she had wanted "something cheerful," and I chose Rabelais's *Gargantua*, firmly convinced that nothing could be more cheerful than this "fearful life story." However, it turned out that Angela found the text barely comprehensible and, for that matter, boring. And that was how, finally, in the kitchen, with a teaspoon of tea in my hand, I became the chief culprit responsible for everything that had offended her gaze that morning—the passengers' bulbous noses, and the bad architecture, the burned-out open spaces, and Renaissance humor. I did not respond to these accusations, however: I restrained myself because I was quite capable of understanding Angela's irrationality. In any case, I would find some way of coming to terms with the sense of guilt she had dumped on me. As for her, she may have peed a lot, but she cried just as much. It was presumably all that water in her thighs, or else she was really finding the seventh month hard going, but all that unpleasantness would disappear once Angela arrived at the end of that exhausting journey, with a wonderful bundle in her arms.

I poured the tea into the cups and milk into a delicate pottery jug that my mother had given us when Angela moved into Molerova Street, I took out the sugar and added the final touch: a smile of reconciliation. "Belgrade's hideous," I agreed. "And maybe Rabelais is boring." Even though I didn't actually think so, I said it out of consideration for Angela's new sensitivity, determined to give in, to accept all the blame. Anyway, who cared about Rabelais? I was resolved to spend hours, if necessary, licking my wounds, wearing the Guilty cap in the punishment corner of our marriage, just not to let Angela upset herself needlessly. I comforted myself with the thought that I would see that she got her comeuppance when the time came, after our son was born and grown up. I swore to myself that when we were both old and gray I would beat her up mercilessly for the wounds she had inflicted over the decades, which I otherwise tended silently, like an animal—Pharaoh and I were alike in that way—licking them in isolation, not dispersing them in barren whining.

And I needed a descendant, as an analgesic/placebo. To that end, making use of the supreme privilege of the male, I had impregnated Angela, although it was possible that she too saw some personal benefit in the whole thing. In any case, her stomach had grown in record time, so much so that her belly button had shot out like a cork, and there were just a couple of months left until that day when an entirely new being—our son!—would step out of her. I was, understandably, proud, but the more her stomach swelled, the more I was at the same time afraid of that mysterious child. I imagined him helpless, and faithful, loyal, then indifferent, and, finally, openly rebellious, determined to evade me! And maybe, when the time came for the rebellion to erupt in him, I would snore loudly every afternoon, without the least embarrassment, and he would hate me, as I had hated my father, through the thin wall interposed between our two bedrooms. Would I be able to understand him when he no longer wished to understand me, or would I cover myself shamefully with the rags of a soured relationship?—that is the crucial question of parenthood.

Angela was calm. She was amusing herself by rolling a joint. Right beside her, I was warming myself with tea, and choking in insoluble dilemmas. What if the child was born cocky? I wondered, already on my guard against some kind of battle that I would not be capable of foreseeing. Would my clumsy novice-father's defense turn out to be an effective protection in such a clinch? Or would we breathe into each other's mouths, my son and I, like two spent boxers, until we both collapsed, weakened by a multitude of low blows?

15

Lazar's Visit

According to some rule that he himself had established, Angela's younger brother, Lazar, came to visit us every Saturday morning. He used to bring an unusual mixture of herbal teas—his own concoction—in a plastic bag secured with a simple red rubber band, and he would drink them very weak, without sugar. As he sat down in his chair (and he chose for himself the stool we used when we had to change a fuse or reach a book from one of the top shelves), he would awkwardly lift the saffron-colored sheet that served as his clothes, and it would billow around his bony knees, revealing his smooth, boyish legs. Lost in an enormous sweater, made with his own hands, of wool as stiff as a dog's hair, he would take off his cap of the same material, with its short tassel. Each time, I would marvel anew at that spectacular moment when his skull gleamed before our eyes. Apart from the neatly tied pigtail at his nape, there was not a single hair on his head. Often, without warning or informing us beforehand, he would read us something from one of the books he hawked from door to door, hardly ever selling any. With a smile of such sincere joy that it was actually a pleasure to listen to him, at least for the first few minutes, he would usually tell us about the three gunas: Virtue, Passion, and Ignorance. I found it interesting that Lazar never even tried to get the better of his obsessive topic, that he did not say to himself: "Next time I'll talk about football!" His discovery absorbed him and his fascination spoke instead of him. He saw himself as endowed with eternal spiritual life. For us, he sometimes glimpsed new forms in the material world: "Say thank you," I chided Angela, who was listening without blinking.

"We didn't expect anything better," Angela would say, rousing herself. She can't say "thank you," even as a joke.

Anyway, we never really went for these outpourings of Lazar's personal philosophy.* That pathetic mush, that lumpy pudding of quotations and adopted visions, a bit from the *Bhagavadgita*, the tail end of the teachings of Sri Srimad A. C. Bhaktivedanta Swami Prabhupada (whom Lazar increasingly called Master Shrila, or even Shrila, carried away by the spontaneous blossoming of a one-sided intimacy), the undigested terminology of *Footsteps of the*

*"Because you know yourselves that trappings do not make a priest," says Rabelais. And again: "how many there are, in monks' habits, who are not priests; while others have wrapped themselves in a Spanish greatcoat, while they are no Spaniards, nor have they the least trace of Spanish courage!"

Lotus, The Consciousness of Krishna, Transcendental Science, the whole stormy fireworks display of his *Knowledge* and our *Unenlightenedness*, along with his always gentle, by now terribly irritating, smile—there, that is what one could gain, at any moment, from that stranger in a Spanish greatcoat, but not a gram in excess.

This time, however, Lazar was more agitated than usual. For starters, he tapped his Reebok sneaker on the parquet (and why Lazar was so inconsistent in the matter of his Reeboks and had not exchanged them for wooden clogs, or sandals made of untreated rope, remained a mystery to me, and for months I could not help tormenting myself with that insoluble problem: what spiritual quality did those shoes possess and what was it that had driven Lazar to retain them as an integral part of his personal costume?). Secondly, he accepted the joint offered him—and he always refused them, except when he was in a state of serious stress. Presumably determined to lose consciousness, he took three brave drags and the light suddenly flared. A violent cough confirmed his lack of routine communion with that great Teacher, and his ears were as red as a schoolboy's. His eyes filled with tears, he sank into his tea, trying to recover. He had a miraculous technique for absorbing salvation and rapid peace from that nauseous liquid. "If you get half a kilo of chickpeas, I can make a really great meal," he said, turning to me, in a voice somewhat altered by his cough, but a second later (when I had intended to reply with an equally autistic comment, whose cause or association only I could know) he turned his timid gaze to Angela, who at that moment, with an anxious expression, was handing him back a blue envelope with his call-up papers and asking in a trembling voice, "And who took it in?"

"No, no. To start with, you don't get it," replied Lazar. "Angela, I think Mom took it in, I *think* it was her, but only because Dad wasn't at home, and she was afraid to refuse. Otherwise, you know her, she wouldn't have."

"Like hell she wouldn't!" Angela screamed so abruptly that Lazar nearly fell off his stool, and she contented herself, after that sudden outburst of Sicilian family fury, with chewing her nails angrily in silence.

"Anyway," Lazar dared to add, "none of it matters. It's a question of karma."

"You haven't told us what you intend to do," I said to him, licking the joint so that it would burn more evenly. However, my words roused the almost dormant Angela, and before Lazar could offer me any kind of answer, she leapt toward me and hissed into my face, "What do you mean 'intend to do'? There's nothing for him to intend. He has to hide." She turned on her heels toward Lazar:

"Lazar, do you understand what I just said? *You have to hide!*"

But Lazar knew how to appear strong, and decisive, just when one least expected it. That's how it was now; exposed to the aggression of Angela's innate verbosity, he simply waited for the sudden incoming tide to recede of its own accord. Motionless on his stool, he cleansed himself with tea, trying to look as though he were not participating in a situation he himself had provoked. Coughing slightly, he refused the joint I handed him, drank another mouthful, and smiled. "Well, actually, I don't know . . ." he said, getting his own back, finally. "There's something to it all. Maybe I will respond."

I went out with him, into the smoky day. We sank into the din without a word. A wedding procession with a pink-faced bride in a white limousine passed us. Somewhere in the distance, packs of dogs were fighting frenziedly. Sweat was pouring from Lazar's armpit onto his robe of orange sheets, because it was unusually hot for late October. We wandered toward the market. Among the vegetables, potatoes, flowers, and all sorts of knickknacks in the flea-market section, we communicated by avoiding each other's eyes. I think that we understood each other better that way, and something else connected us at that moment: whatever he said, Lazar was afraid of the war, he wasn't altogether indifferent. But who could possibly have thought that I was not afraid? I could see clearly that the circle around me was narrowing. More and more people were being sucked into that whirlpool. One day, I thought, they would bang on my door as well, and then my knees, like those of so many others in recent months, would start knocking.

I must have looked foolish in my pathetic impotence at that moment, and yet I was not ashamed to mock Lazar. There, among the potatoes, I weighed up on an imaginary scale the prospect of participation in the war, and the alternative—military prison, for failure to respond to the draft or desertion, which could only be avoided by going abroad without delay. That was why, at that same instant, I made the decision that I should never be ironical toward my wife's poor younger brother, whom the peasant stall-holders were looking at with suspicion because of his conspicuous clothes and hairstyle. Carried along by this positive wave of compassion, I tried to catch his attention, to smile at him sincerely, benignly, to express my friendliness. I did manage somehow to meet his eye, but I did not receive anything like a smile in return. Lazar simply squinted at me with his penetrating cat's eyes, pretending not to understand my sudden need for partnership in misfortune, he was just paying me back in kind. He never was a saint.

His worldly malice roused me. I dragged him into a sandwich bar on the edge of the marketplace. "Let's get a sandwich," I suggested, and I think that Lazar had already seen through my plan, because he swallowed nervously. "Not for me, thanks," he barely managed to say, "but you—go ahead . . ." From the whole vast array, which included four vegetarian options, I chose a beef-salad sandwich. I offered Lazar a bite as well. "Beef's terrific," I said, my mouth full. Lazar's revulsion was my spiritual food that October, even if it brought inexorably closer whatever he believed I had coming to me.

A Sketch About Executors and Commanders

Anyway, there's no punishment, or reward either. There are no transgressions, or merit. I knew that then as well, in the market, with the agitated Lazar beside me. Natural law is an inscription that we can decipher only partially. Jesus Christ was the victim of his own clumsy policy; God had been searching, in vain, for some time, for a new Messiah, in an endeavor to send us the following message: *There, now* *you can do anything, all is permitted.* From the vantage point I call "Yugoslavia, October 1991," this notion sounds demoralizing, but Swedenborg was right when he said that God does not judge, because He loves everyone equally, while a man settles for one or the other of the two eternal kingdoms, since he is the bearer of his own Good or Evil.* The postmortal segregation (like natural law itself, for that matter) is nothing other than a desire for harmony, as the most agreeable of all states. And the law of nature itself is partially founded on segregation, but it is only heavenly segregation that is absolute. An impenetrable membrane divides the two existing camps and does not interfere with them. This membrane is loved and respected equally by both camps. They need it, because Heaven is to the Evil just what Hell is to the Good: a loathsome, contaminated place. They are not thrown into the lower kingdom, but—contrary to received wisdom, and in keeping with their genuine nature, of which it is possible they were not aware during their lifetime—they chose it themselves. They do not complain in that wasteland, they do not suffer at all, they are not exposed—again, contrary to earthly preju-

*Emanuel Swedenborg, *Heaven and Hell*, Part III, *Hell*: "The Lord does not throw anyone into Hell, that is the work of the Holy Ghost."

dices—to any kind of torture on the part of demons, because they are themselves demons; nor do they long for Heaven, and according to their former brethren, they are more likely to feel mockery than envy. In the kingdom of conspirators, murderers, and politicians, they seethe in their own black satisfaction.

All of the above explains why, from my early youth and my first encounter with Swedenborg, I felt such disdain for all distorted ideas about consuming or not consuming beef salad, pork, alcohol, drugs; why I refused to be weighed down with such burning questions of civilization as the right to abortion, the moral problem of fur coats and leather shoes, the question of the limits of sexual freedom, or the greenhouse effect; why I allowed myself not to know how Orthodox believers crossed themselves and how Catholics did it, and at the same time not to be a convinced atheist either. In fact, because of Swedenborg, I was disgusted by that whole catalogue of manifestations of different dogmas (which, of course, included the one to which Lazar had so naïvely donated his whole being) whose only aim was to hide from us the great truth that God strives and struggles to impose on us. Here is that truth, for all true believers: *The essence of our whole predilection is established in us, despite us, before we are born.* Choice does not actually exist, since it is a question of a simple implant. Isn't that demoralizing, and splendid? In that sense, we are all Executors—like a serial killer who kills although he is repelled by violence, since the poor man is nothing other than an executioner in the service of his own Evil—and when the Commander is elusive it is the Executors who are punished. When, once and for all, our laws learn to recognize the Commander inside the Executor, and to eliminate him, insofar as that appears to be essential, and at the same time not to harm the Executor, then he will be looked upon, with expressions of the deepest sympathy, as a besieged being, and our progressive legislature will grant us the status of demigods, and something in that magnificent balance will collapse. But we are still a long way from getting a handle on that natural law. The balance of Heaven and Hell (according to Swedenborg) is stable.

I'm afraid I'm being too harsh (particularly in the light of the ensuing events, for which the reader must wait a little longer, and which constitute this book), so I simply put this forward as a thesis: our Saturday meeting in October made it more than clear that out of those seven or nine, or however many, openings on Lazar's body, a quite different Lazar was beginning to emerge. It would have suited his theoretical convictions to be disgusted by any armed conflict, to have stated (with that smile), "Well, I'd rather not take part," and even to have gone and repeated that same sentiment before some kind of military commission, insofar as such a body exists. However, Lazar did none of that, and the crust of his faith—a faith expressed through a dry radicalism—was shown to be painfully thin. Just underneath it there hid a Commander, who had even said, in Lazar's name: "Well, actually, I don't know . . . There's something to it all. Maybe I will respond," attracted by a childish cowboys-and-Indians perception of the Serbo-Croat mutual slaughter. If that was how it was, I thought on my way back from the market, then at the front (under pressure from the Commander, who would have assumed complete control to get him there) Lazar would not have any major problems, he'd replace his mixture of teas with brandy, his chickpeas with roast pork from a Slavonian sow blown apart by a grenade; if that was how it was, then Lazar would discover himself subscribing to one of the passions on offer out there as local specialties, he'd feel rapture (instead of a pang of conscience) when his first victim fell under his aim, he would be Arjuna in the mud and filth of the Pannonian *Kuruksetra*. At that moment, as I made my way home from the market with shreds of beef still stuck between my teeth, I discovered that I was afraid—of Lazar. It all fitted into my terrifying theory. And Lazar himself had often indicated the same thing. In keeping with his favorite theory about states of being, the participants in these little wars of plunder belonged to a grouping of human beings who lived in profound, unforgivable Ignorance. According to that theory, they could expect (as he could himself, since he had sworn by his Virtue and then done the opposite) the brief, transient lives of worms, vermin, plankton, or bacteria, just enough to gain some sense.*

The Lazar in whom we believed (and who had in fact never existed), that Lazar would never have agreed to such a thing. But perhaps it just suited that 100 percent spiritual Executor to believe, in order to follow the Commander's plan with greater ease, that, despite the merit he had achieved, he would prefer the peaceful, harmonious life of a dandelion to the spiritual existence he had been promised, in the form of a fragment of skin from Krishna's ankle?

Why Angela's Courage Scares Me

But still, to be honest, all my conclusions about Lazar were reached at that small height that is the privilege of the story-

*But even here it is not clear what a bacterium could do to help itself; what should it do, during its existence, in order, at the next distribution, to be certain of promotion to a higher level?

teller. In the thick of it, in October, I was not half as surprised at Lazar as I was at his and Angela's parents. I could not understand why Vida and Mihailo, whom, despite all the illogicalities of their characters, I considered sensible people, had agreed to accept the call-up papers, which at that time were so petrifying people that no one would take them in his hands at any price, let alone sign for them (which they had done wholeheartedly). Beside herself with fury, Angela called them collaborators. And she was right. It was not hard for me to imagine them serving coffee to the soldiers who had brought the papers—they had always enjoyed the role of a pleasant married couple. And the fact that they became collaborators through their foolishness, rather than any sinister impulse, did not vindicate them.

Then the question of my wife began to intrigue me. What would Angela have done in a similar situation? Put on the spot, would she have known what to do, I wondered, how would she have reacted? None of all the possible answers cheered me. If I knew my wife, I concluded, she would have exploited this exceptional opportunity to hurl all sorts of insults into the faces of those issuing the papers (just as, a couple of months earlier, swollen with pregnancy, she had climbed onto the improvised stage at a peace rally and made a fiery political speech, while I sat mortified in the garden of a nearby café). And it was possible that she would have slammed the door in their faces. Scandalized by such a demonstration of hostility, the drafters would probably have retreated, but they would soon have come back—with reinforcements! And I shook with fear at such a prospect. Perhaps they would forget me, or write me off—a barren hope, but anything was possible in a country that was floundering like this. I was immediately overcome by an unusual feverishness. Faced with the constant possibility that an irate Angela might stomp on their already excessively stomped-on corns, if I did not at once take some action to anticipate it, I would live from then on in the company of an unanswerable, dementing question: What would be left for me in the future? "Angela?" I resolved to test her general mood. At the same time, I trembled with anxiety, but Angela did not seem to notice. "Angela, what would you do if, say, they came for me, as they did for Lazar?"

"I guess I'd slam the door in their faces," said Angela quickly and petulantly, after a second's thought. Preoccupied with a television program, she missed seeing me pass out, behind her, from the shock.

We went to sleep early that evening, in front of the television. A kindly bluish ray trembled over us. Throughout the satellite channels, our boys were slaughtering each other for all they were worth. Angela wrapped her leg around me; although, in the meantime, I had regained consciousness, I had even washed, I was still swallowing numerous lumps of accumulated fear; her thigh was heavy, but somehow we snuggled under one blanket that smelled of naphthalene. What could I do in the silence, other than weep soundlessly?

Voices from the Torrent

On the other hand, it sometimes seemed to me that I hadn't much justification for such unbecoming behavior. What's an ordinary war to me? I would wonder then. Ever since I'd gotten used to adulthood, I had lived at the center of a long-drawn-out Armageddon. People around me kept on dying in the most incredible ways, and in the late eighties and early nineties this process intensified to such a degree that I simply could not keep in my head the essential, if melancholy, Statistics of the Dead. A whole armada of potential Angelas kept on buzzing ceaselessly in it.*

*See Appendix 1, "A Compilation of Deaths: 1989, 1990, 1991."

It was even impossible to mourn all those who disappeared as they perhaps deserved. All too often, not even a full month would have passed since the last of the deaths when here was a new victim hovering over our heads for a moment and then vanishing forever. Once I was an amateur, but these increasingly frequent deaths had made me an expert in all types of burial. I had just begun to worry that I was going to get hardened prematurely to all that when the war in Croatia broke out, and bequeathed me a valuable, if nebulous, lesson: all individual deaths, taken together, represented just the (private) overture to a (public) classical bloody tragedy that, like every genuine tragedy, was concerned with the great theme of war between peoples. The really nasty fact was that, at the time I'm writing of, the play had actually only just begun. More precisely, we were witnessing the setting up of the first act, and we had already had enough. The lack of basic conventions was troubling. We hoped fruitlessly that we would soon catch sight of the final curtain, we longed for a happy ending, but we knew that the deus ex machina would not soon come down from his mechanical cloud, to separate the opponents and distribute justice in equal proportions. It was an extremely disturbing realization: *There's still a whole lot more death to come.* In the end, we shall learn to live with it, and won't be so afraid of it as we once were. It'll become tedious.

But in a way, that was all TV. The real world never

offers the protection of a definite conclusion. It's true that by October 1991 there weren't nearly as many wartime deaths in my life as peacetime ones (that is, up until then only one person who was relatively close to me had died in that war), but then the war had not lasted nearly as long as the safe embrace of peace.

The first person to drop out of the game was called Ivan. I spent two whole years in his company, cutting classes at secondary school. I liked him, but not enough to keep up with him after I had scraped by and completed my hated education, while he was forced to repeat the final year. So, twelve years after our last shared memory, Ivan must have felt cheated when, on a farm near Erdut, as he was having a morning pee, wondering sleepily what to do with the two hundred jars of pickles he had stolen from his Hungarian host, he was surprised by an explosion. I say that because I am sure that he had imagined a somewhat more substantial role for himself than the one he managed to play. As it was, after this episode there wasn't enough of Ivan left for even one of those two hundred jars, which he had intended to turn into cash.

As for Dejan, that was a bit sadder because I genuinely loved Dejan. We had gone to swimming training together, although he was already sick of those frequent, monotonous sessions. He swam because his father wanted him to, but he himself dreamed of becoming a drummer.

Years later (when he was actually too old for a beginner), he played in a band called GSG 9, after the elite West German antiterrorist commando corps. They looked great then, bare to the waist, muscular, hairless, sweaty, and serious, surrounded by computers and strobe lights, and while two of these guys sampled reports of mass deaths and great catastrophes, Wagner, Stravinsky, and the sounds of cities being shelled, Dejan, shaved bald, sweating more than any of them, played his set of drums, standing, as though he were inflicting punishment on them. Despite their unpronounceable name, GSG 9 were extremely ambitious—Dejan was their motivating force, he was the only person I knew who expressed the serious intention of doing something with his life. His hands were covered with blisters from practicing, he no longer had any fingerprints—the tips of his fingers were completely smooth. Then they cut a record with an independent producer in Maribor, and in time their concerts became more and more popular. In Belgrade, Ljubljana, Zagreb, Rijeka, Skoplje, Trieste, Vienna, wherever GSG 9 were playing, their audience consisted mostly of thin little urban girls in Doc Martens who were regularly high on large doses of tranquilizers.

All of that was, of course, brought to an abrupt end, and during the late summer and early autumn of 1991 cast into the realm of a deeply mourned past. Dejan had to try to say farewell to his right arm, and when I visited him in the Military Hospital, where they had amputated it, he was getting by with the other one. We had a smoke in the bathroom, and then we dragged ourselves back to his room. He stretched out on the bed. He turned on the radio, but switched it off right away, blushing for some reason. I drew a chair up to the head of his bed and sat down. We talked nonsense, for the most part. He remembered my T-shirt with the enormous white star across the chest and the inscription BRIGADE ROSSE, which I hadn't wanted to sell to him despite his pestering me for years, because I had gotten it as a present. I had the impression that he felt terribly uncomfortable without that arm. He behaved as though he had suddenly stumbled, naked, into a formal reception. He kept covering himself up to his chin, insisting that he was cold. But the whole time, quite against his will, the hand on his remaining arm kept leaping out of the covers, gesticulating wildly. "I shouldn't have given you that smoke," I said, in a rather overblown joke, although, really, I shouldn't have.

I still remember, because it was touching, Dejan hoping, throughout my visit, that when he got out, the October sun that he could see through the window would still be waiting for him. "Sure it will," I replied stupidly, shrugging my shoulders. I hoped that, without my preaching, Dejan would understand what was *really* in store for him: heaps of Balkan mud, encroaching November, expressions full of sympathy, and nostalgic encounters with the alleyways of the deceived capital city.

And, in brief, that would be that. It is true that there were three others, at that time, but I had no information about them. While they perished as they peed, while they had their limbs separated from them, while they gambled with horror, I was suffocating in my daily routine, and it happened that days would go by without my giving them a thought. I intended, from time to time, to telephone their parents, girlfriends, or wives, but I would recoil from the receiver each time I picked it up, and put it straight down again. All of this, put in a nicer way: I was wavering. I scrutinized our relations. What, I wondered, what if, for one reason or another, we were never as close as it had seemed?

What I mean is that things were bad, but not so bad that they could not have been a great deal worse. At that time, the war had not yet hit us in the face with the knot of human innards that was to come; it crushed us in a wiser way. Our telephone went silent, while once we could not find a moment's peace from it. The majority of our friends were far away, beyond the borders of the country. In the demanding process of trying to survive, they were without telephones, or spare time, or money—in any case, they rarely called. From time to time a postcard would reach us from Budapest, Prague, Copenhagen, Casablanca, Athens, Amsterdam, London, from all those splendid places, and they were genuinely welcome, those postcards, but still, it was hard to resist the impression that they had all been written by the same person. They were filled with meager scrawlings, and somehow the message always seemed to be the same, regardless of the local conditions: "I can't get work," "I'm earning a bit," "it's hard," "but I'm OK," "I'm coping," etc., etc.*

Many people swore that they had not run away from the war. Some maintained that their departure had absolutely nothing to do with the war; they left because they felt like it.

"You notice a difference," Angela said to me once. "Before they used to die, and now they go away . . ." I smiled. They died less of late, it was true, but there was no real difference: we would still see someone off every couple of weeks, and soon have to get over their loss. Nineteen ninety-one introduced a new activity into our lives. We invented new friends, or we spent time with the friends of our exiled friends, or sometimes we renewed contact with acquaintances from long ago. There was a certain sense to it all—we no longer distinguished our real social wishes

*See Appendix 2, "Chronicle of the Escapees: 1990, 1991."

from our expert feats of adaptability. We practiced, throughout that whole year, a new kind of tolerance, and we mastered it: people whom we had previously ignored became welcome guests. We competed when the telephone rang, and I was faster than Angela, especially in the autumn, since she had put on weight, and her breasts had grown, and her stomach kept getting in her way, and she shuffled clumsily as she ran.

I could wrap myself and warm myself in concern with the Vanished, like layers of skin (of which there were never enough), but here is a collective image. In March of that year, pointless demonstrations were held, and many people mentioned in this book, and many more of us besides, stood pressed together in an urban bottleneck, under the yellow lights of the main street. How foolish we were, and comical! We shouted, we protested, we were terribly angry, but in the final reckoning, we scored far more own goals than real goals. Then, only a couple of months later, this is what happened to us: some of us were mugging on the blue obituary notices stuck crookedly on telegraph poles, some were going to lengthy therapy sessions in hospital, some were writing postcards from abroad, some were deriving infantile pleasure from those postcards . . . And I wonder, what on earth were we doing, wasting all that time in the streets, only to allow all this to happen to us? It was hard enough for us, that autumn, to make out whether we actually existed or not. The process of finishing us off lasted only a few months: we were pummeled by a blitzkrieg of low blows. In the October of which I am writing, in the March that was in store for me, halfway between one and the other, I was more afraid than I had been disgusted in the March before. I was afraid that in the coming March I would see us all in some bad portrait, and that terrible holes would gape among us, and that between all those hollows there would be desperately few of us, and that we would not know what to say to one another, and that we would walk about in a place that had been deprived of all sense, praying to God to disperse us all as quickly and painlessly as possible, with bad weather, rough looks, curses, water cannons, and rubber truncheons.

I don't know even now how to explain what it was that happened to us, but I am pretty sure that some destiny we had all forgotten about had been fulfilled. And that can happen, too. For something yelled, and in an instant it had created a torrent and swept us away. It was a biblical experience. Intermittently, in that whirlpool like a turbulent river, a head would rise to the surface, a helpless limb would stretch upward to aim a feeble kick at the swollen buttocks of the sky, sodden eyes snatched at views that were ever more distant, from one day to the next, hands flew out like strange beings to seize things that had never been there in any case. As time went on, there were ever fewer of us in that whirlpool, and we were all ranting, in agitated voices, about the foam through which one sank, which offered no support, through which one was being buffeted grotesquely, which did not nourish, which could not quench one's thirst, which was of no use for anything, which had no color, or taste, or smell, which was false and deceitful, and undermined everything precious and logical. Not listening to one another, we bleated about the airy lava that generalized and leveled us, we talked about solubility, about disintegration, about the last moments of a sick world—the proprietor of a colony of voracious viruses. Our stories were different, our experience contradictory—as if that were even remotely relevant! The foam in which we were drowning would in any case corrode, merge, swallow all of them. And in the end, all that would be left of that terrible pain and suffering would be just one insignificant bubble hovering in the air, and then it too would burst.

PART II

November 1991

My Drug-Dealer Wife—Lazar Wasn't Joking, But Neither Was Angela—On the Month of Dying—How I Fell in Love with Dejan All Over Again—A Relative, and My Total Nosedive, from Which I Would Emerge in One Piece, Endowed with a Unique Moral—About My Mother and Father

My Drug-Dealer Wife

The person responsible for Angela's and my meeting was Petar. The process of establishing our relationship was, however, more complex than that—and more wonderful too. At that time, all of Angela's friends were actually friends of the man she was going out with, who had been in prison in Switzerland for some time by then. They weren't a team of dangerous criminals but Belgrade dealers, most of whom were students, and some were already engaged in quite reputable social activities. On the other hand, all of my friends made use of their services, including the aforementioned Petar. They used to spend hours of their lives on city squares, huddled together, stamping their feet, clutching their money in their pockets, waiting for one of Angela's friends to appear as arranged. The latter enjoyed the dealer's unique privilege of being able to saunter up nonchalantly, with no apology, a good half hour or more late, or simply not to turn up, if they didn't feel like it. They were masters of the goods they offered, while my friends were its slaves. They would arrive at the agreed-upon meeting place ten or fifteen minutes before the appointed hour, determined to wait, out of fear that, just this once, the dealer would come on time. Were that to happen (according to my friends' vivid paranoia), seeing that there were no customers at the agreed-upon spot, the dealer would simply go away, and the customer would fall into enduring disfavor. It was all stupid, of course, because dealers simply cannot come on time, but such was the nature of the relationship. Nothing could be done about it.

With time, Angela learned most of the principles involved in her friends' business, and she decided to go into action herself. She began to take their customers away, because she was an innovator: she wasn't late, or at least not very late, and her rates were reasonable. Angela's friends took heroin with anything at all, and in cynical proportions. It's true that Angela shorted them on the weights, but what she sold was reliably pure and good. Angela turned out to be an exceptional pupil, unlike me, who, despite many attempts, never acquired *my* friends' rather less lucrative skills. Even at that time, when I was traveling meekly, every morning, from the flat in Molerova Street, first by tram, then by bus, to my office on Banovo Brdo, I suffered from indigestion and gastritis. In my free time, I used to have friends over, smoke pot, and write; at work I issued dispatch notes, filled out forms, did battle with ledgers, feeling entirely indifferent to all of it. Angela lived with her parents and brother in a three-bedroom flat in New Belgrade, where she didn't like being. She had too much time on her hands, but also a lot of money, earned, in a sense, honestly. It's true that Angela was engaged in a highly criminalized trade (which was not overseen by the Retailers' Union, but did have its own undisputed rules, and the structure of a genuine market, although the values of that trade were tangential to those of the official one). Still, she was a more honest worker than me. I did only as much as I was supposed to do in my job, while she tried to advance hers. She was probably the only dealer in the city who would approve a week's loan. She understood intuitively that it was best if she approved it for all her customers (always, admittedly, in the guise of exceptional circumstances), and this goodness was repaid with elegant gestures of deep friendship.

When Angela and I used to meet after I'd finished work, in town, or at my place, she would treat me to lavish quantities of horse or crack, ecstasy or coke—Angela had everything in enormous quantities. When I was high, I used to tell her about the women I worked with: a bunch of good-humored unmarried girls with bad hairdos and fat, maternal knees, whose round imperfection I would wonder at aloud, whose inadequacies, in those long toxic monologues, I would idealize to such an extent that if I had been catapulted too high by euphoria, I would sometimes think it would be quite satisfying to exist in the form of one of their intimate sponges, dildos, or tampons—to exist, that is, as nothing but an auxiliary device that keeps you company when you're alone and is discarded after use.

Insofar as she was able to hold up her head, which used to keep drooping, Angela enjoyed these stories—at least as much as I enjoyed the privilege of spending time with girls like that. In the gulf where the two of us had met (although we came from opposite sides of it, and in that sense, we embodied the living myth of the world's great lovers), those girls—decent, warm, and modest, forever smiling—shone like little angels with trumpets and violins, those decorative creatures that adorn the edges of touched-up photographs capturing scenes of some long-since-yellowed childhood.

Of course, Angela had her great themes as well. In lazy tones, she would talk about her "fiancé," incarcerated some distance from here, where he was sentenced to remain until 1995, which meant that his position in Angela's value system (which I understood better than anyone) was in rapid flux. The style of Angela's anecdotes was unusual, demonstrating an early Hellenistic narrative procedure. The characterology of her hero was stunted. He had fought in every situation with apparent indifference, as though his actions had been governed by the will of a higher authority. Although she talked about him often, not one single fact ever surfaced that could have given me the slightest impression of him, so it was not surprising that my real fear of this shadow over our relationship followed me right up to our wedding day. It appeared as I was watching Angela, jubilant in her short wedding dress the color of face powder, dancing a waltz with my father. What would that brute say, I wondered, when he turned up here, in that distant year of 1995, fortified by many years of prison regime, furious and strong, to claim his sacred male right to Angela, and found her in the company of some man (me!) whose child Angela would certainly have had by then? When I confided my fears to Angela that night, at the height of the party we had thrown in Molerova Street for our friends, she smiled sweetly at me, ecstatic with coke and champagne. "But he's much shorter than you," she said, describing that international criminal for the first time, "and . . . and . . . he's very nice—you'd really like him, I'm sure, and he you. You like the same music, and he reads a lot, just like you; I mean, he couldn't hurt a fly."

That's how that was settled. We spent our honeymoon in Rome, and then, in grand style, Angela moved in with me, with her cat, Pharaoh, whom her mother and father could hardly wait to see the back of.

The day after she moved in, Angela made a truly miraculous decision. With the dedication of people who faithfully follow a diet to the grave, she stopped using any kind of opiate, so as to clean out her organism for her forthcoming pregnancy. I shall never forget the hell of the first weeks of that long process. Angela sweated, she couldn't settle anywhere, she would slam doors over the slightest thing, she chased Pharaoh around the house with a slipper for no obvious reason, she complained of backache, nausea, and pains in her joints, but she did not give up. The only thing she had for breakfast, lunch, and dinner was Benzedrine. But we did smoke pot, from morning to night. My friends, Angela's customers, turned out to be real monsters. They besieged our flat because, after buying from Angela, they didn't feel like going back to her friends; we were sure that the siege was being carried out according to a carefully worked-out plan because they literally did not leave us alone, and when they finally realized that all their endeavors were fruitless, in their despair they began to hate me. They insisted that I was responsible for Angela's decision to straighten herself out, a decision that also determined her unilateral break with all her business connections. However, Angela didn't take the slightest notice of them, nor of the fact that, without her regular income, we were becoming more and more penniless. She cleansed herself for a whole year, and I have the impression that she got pregnant the first time she let me ejaculate inside her. When she announced the news to me, in an exalted voice, I didn't protest. I wanted an heir, and as far as Angela was concerned, all the moves described above were proof of her sincere desire, once and for all, to meet up with her true nature, to become what she had in fact always wanted to be—*a housewife.*

Lazar Wasn't Joking, But Neither Was Angela

For a long time Lazar did not belong to the growing collection of our regular topics of conversation, and it was only when Angela had moved in with me that he decided to impose himself, and so became a regular part of our marital routine. His Saturday visits were a kind of social compassion; he used to visit us the way a legend of the stage and screen would visit a down-and-out friend from childhood in an old-people's home, as though he were filling the time reserved for him out of pure decency. After three or four visits arranged in advance, always at the same time on the same day, he created in us a kind of conditioned reflex, so that if one of the two of us were to suggest some other arrangement for Saturday mornings, the other would respond, not without a certain satisfaction: "But how can we? What about Lazar?" We were afraid that he might be hurt by our absence.

Lazar's apparent fragility was a substitute for the charm he lacked. Angela was particularly sensitive to that fragility. "You don't know what it means to be an older sister," she said once, in a voice full of emotion, and I found it comical. But it soon turned out that I really did not know. Angela's advanced sense of responsibility for Lazar dated from his birth, when she was four years old. From that early age she had taken upon herself the difficult task of being his guide along the untrodden paths of growing up. Behind that lay a quite conscious intention, the weapon of pure hatred—to transform the only life subordinate to hers into an intolerable irritation. Even after such a confession, I was no nearer understanding how that small being could have known exactly what to do with an even smaller being! And then, despite everything, regardless of the motives that in any case did not exceed the standard jealousy of the first child toward the second, it had turned out that it wasn't as easy as it might seem to vex a person. According to Angela, torn by frequent pangs of conscience and onrushes of flaming shame, the contradictions of such a relationship were appalling. Even though she bullied and abused him, according to an obscure need that, over the years, turned into a practiced routine, she remembered loving him intensely, although she endeavored to express it through contrary, typically sisterly reactions—accusations and fabrications, lies and slander, contempt and scheming. Molding him freely, like a lump of Plasticine, she did not expect him to notice immediately the results of her years of effort (and she had pinched him when he was still in his cradle, pushed him over in passing when he was learning to walk, beaten him on the soles of his feet with a hairbrush when their parents weren't in sight; later she had shoved his wretched freckled head into a bowl full of icy water, chased him with a bread knife in an apparent upsurge of motiveless fury, tripped him up in places where a fall could have been fatal, goaded him into pushing their mother's knitting needles into electric sockets, putting his hand on a hot plate, shoving beans into his nose and ears, and jumping from the roof of their father's garage onto a heap of rubble and broken bricks). She was rewarded for these efforts after some fifteen years when one day, to everyone's consternation, with only Angela having a valid explanation (which, however, she refused to share with anyone), Lazar suddenly left school, and decided to expose his body to all kinds of trials. He did so elementally, without a clearly defined aim, in a frenzied search for a suitable ideology. From that period his chest was striped with scars from the razor blades with which he slit his skin, and his pale hands were forever disfigured with the dark imprints of burns from cigarettes extinguished on them. But, as is often the way, someone did come along and present him with a framework in which to operate. Lazar was furnished with his first task, which went roughly as follows: *to deny completely the bodily sack of Bile, Mucus, and Air, in order that, within it, the Embryo of a new Lazar should be conceived.*

At that point, Angela could have withdrawn to one side, with a clear conscience, adopting a gently ironic attitude. But she didn't. The next phase of her Pygmalion-like activity, despite her ever more frequent and painful doubts about the result, consisted in a constant bombardment of reproaches and insults, chipping and rubbing away any remaining nuggets of self-confidence, which he could have possessed only in crumbs by then. All that made the wretched, surface Lazar—*the Executor*—cringe and sulk, but in fact it barely affected him. Hidden deep within him, invisible to most, but not to Angela's subconscious, Lazar—*the Commander*—felt great, for in fact each of her actions actually nourished and strengthened him.

"But why on earth did you do it all?" I asked, staggered, but Angela looked at me as though I were a hostile animal, and burst into tears. What could I know about the whole thing? Perhaps, by confiding in me, Angela had assigned too much importance to her actions, in the light of events I shall relate later. Her tears were frequent, but sometimes I doubted them. At other times, her pain would be convincing; sometimes I cried with her, out of solidarity. I recognized all the good in my wife—she was the woman I loved; I ran my fingers through her hair; at that time, there was a cosmonaut floating in the depths of Angela, ready to leave the mother ship: *our son.*

Nevertheless, I should have dealt with her pain earlier, in time, and not when it was all over. I ought to have examined it when, instead of the usual Saturday Lazar, with books under his arm and his pigtail, we received a telegram in which he informed us of his decision to respond to his call-up papers after all, justifying it, again, more as a function of karma than of personal desire. Reading the curt message several times over, Angela rubbed the palm of her hand over her stomach. "I could use some horse," she said in a conciliatory tone, with a barely audible sigh (that was the first time she had mentioned heroin since we had lived together), but her hand, as she laid the folded telegram on the table, was shaking uncontrollably.

"Perhaps he's changed his mind?" I said, offering an unconvincing option, for temporary lack of anything better, and that redirected the whole negative charge that had accumulated in Angela onto me. That violent quarrel and mutual recriminations could have made us spend the next few days in offended silence, avoiding each other, had the mild, sunny afternoons not thawed us.

On one such afternoon we visited Angela's parents. They were polite, as ever. They behaved as though nothing unusual were going on—I suppose they had the best of intentions, not wanting to test Angela's temperament, which they knew well—but their approach was quite misguided, because it was precisely that feigned ignorance that infuriated Angela. Apart from that, she owed them a showdown in connection with their having accepted Lazar's call-up papers and signed for them. Her parents didn't expect anything different because their experience had already suggested that their daughter usually visited them when she felt like a fight. And so, when Angela, in a calm tone of voice, broached the subject of Lazar's departure for the front, I trembled, but her parents were a sight: like marathon runners in their starting positions, they were tense, braced, and very apprehensive. They rebuffed her initial accusations in unison, in short sentences, trying not to provoke her; by taking turns to answer, they allowed each other short breathing spaces to gather their thoughts. I had observed contests like this several times already, and they were sometimes really comical, although, as a rule, they would end in major family tragedies that were usually short-lived. Quite simply, they didn't take it all to heart. But the supreme experience was to find myself once again in the center of that whirlpool, hearing Angela shrieking, "You make me sick! You make me sick! You've always hated Lazar, you've always hated me! When did you ever help us, in anything?!" and so on, until Vida began talking at the same time, in a vain attempt to outshout her: "What is it? What do you want? You should be ashamed of yourself! I signed the papers, so what! What business is it of yours, anyway? Besides, Lazar told me to sign, if you really want to know, that's right, because I'm usually at home, and he's not! There you are! What do you know about what I think about it all, shame on you!" and at the same time Mihailo turned to me: "Hey, listen, it's no joking matter. Just down the road two guys were arrested for avoiding military service. What's got into you, children!"

As a rule, in these quarrels there would be a decisive moment resulting from a lapse in the otherwise stable defense *Mihailo–Vida*. This time it was Vida who made the lapse, when she admitted carelessly that she had no idea where on the front line Lazar was, adding sorrowfully, while Mihailo tried to silence her with a glance: "He promised to write!" Although Vida bit her tongue immediately, blue in the face, conscious of her fatal mistake, Angela did not miss the opportunity to launch a brutal attack. With her enormous stomach, she leapt to her feet; standing with her legs apart, massive as she was, she looked like an aggressive bulldog ready for a scrap. Yelling the most terrible insults and curses, she collected her things from around the house, and gathering up her hair in front of the mirror in the hall, she combed it furiously. She always did that when she felt that the quarrel had reached its peak, so as to be sure that she would have the last word by making the end of her oration coincide with her exit from her parents' flat, which she left furiously and violently, as though she were never coming back.

It was even more unusual how, in that house, other activities would get swept into the quarrels, but that was the family's style. For instance, this time, while the battle was in full swing, we were given a considerable quantity of cookies wrapped in foil, and when everything began to slide inexorably downhill, and it was clear that a new family schism could not be avoided, Mihailo took it upon himself to soothe the situation, just as Angela was letting fly oath after oath and Vida was weeping bitterly over the dishes in the kitchen, by suddenly appearing in his new slippers—showing them off proudly and drawing particular attention to the side fastening. His effort did not bear fruit, as everything had already been said. Angela was noticeably flagging and running out of inspiration, but still, determined to conclude the attack she had launched in a spectacular manner, she suddenly did something she had never tried before. She hurled the cookies to the ground, so that the foil split and the brittle squares scattered over the carpet, staining it with jam and ground walnuts. As I stood astounded, she grabbed me by the hand, and before I could manage to say goodbye to her parents, whom I liked a lot, she dragged me into the hall, slamming the door violently as she left.

On the Month of Dying

And all that time, November was devouring its own heart. Dubrovnik, shelled and leading the news in October, had been replaced by mind-blowing Vukovar vignettes. Angela wept, resting her chin on the arm of the sofa, as she watched splinters of the devastated settlements on the Danube and Vuka, in the background of the rustic-featured wartime TV reporter's saccharine outpourings. Winding diagonally across our screen, columns of numb figures who had just dragged themselves out of their cellars after a hundred days stared blankly; gray-haired children smiled shyly at us, showing their broken teeth; the body of a man leaning his head against the wall of something that might once have been his home, an undignified heap of plaster piled on his head; a soldier burned to the bone, the black mass, still hot, smoking hideously. We saw also a young woman with half a head, refugees freezing in sports arenas, the corpses of people and animals strewn in the streets of a shattered town where some men were driving around in jeeps, their job done, and we shuddered with fear that, in that madness, we might catch sight of Lazar, drunk, unruly, and unshaven, like the whole crowd of liberators.

So we turned off the television. We realized that we were, quite simply, incapable of dealing with such scenes. Weary of horror, aware that getting used to death would take longer and hurt more than we had imagined in our shameful gullibility and arrogance, and increasingly anxious about Lazar's fate, we comforted ourselves with thoughts of the New Year. The poverty we had sunk into was unbearable. Things had never been worse. Luckily, we had the certainty of the child to take our minds off it, otherwise we would have snapped at each other, for sure. As it was, we would sometimes walk through town, bargaining for tiny garments or toys—we simply didn't have the wherewithal for anything more substantial—and the shop assistants would see us out, thanking us in their western accents. But that therapy couldn't heal the wounds opened by the scenes from Vukovar. Angela began shaking her head reproachfully. Once, when she was in the kitchen and didn't know I was watching, she slapped her stomach angrily, then in horror slumped heavily onto a chair, sobbing. I know that I should have stepped in at that moment, and our love would have blossomed forever, but I didn't: I just crept spinelessly back into the living room, on tiptoe, so that Angela wouldn't know of my chance presence. I was overwhelmed by sadness that evening as she did her maternity exercises, more zealously than usual. Lying on her back, she raised one leg after the other into the air. I came up to her from behind, knelt down, and kissed her on the neck. Suddenly, as though she were about to fall, she clung to me. She held me tight. And, it is true, there was an abyss gaping beneath us.

The next day, or perhaps the day after that, when I came home from work, Angela met me with shining eyes—she had news of Lazar. For several days now, while I was at the office, she had embarked on fruitless searches through the Belgrade barracks where conscripts were held temporarily, before their final allocation to the war zones. She told me that she had also gone to the War Office, but they had claimed not to know anything except that Lazar had responded properly to his call-up papers, satisfying all their requirements for information. Lazar's friends, or whatever they called themselves, were no more helpful. When Angela visited them in their Temple, they smiled broadly, sang "Hare Krishna," treated her to a vegetarian lunch that she enjoyed, but she left them knowing more about their beads and hairdos than about her brother. Perhaps they really didn't know anything about him, or perhaps they had rejected him; it's perfectly possible that they saw him as one of those wavering novices who easily succumb, and were ashamed of him.

And then, on the bus, weary from her visit, no longer knowing where to turn, Angela met someone she knew, and this person told her that her friend, or relation, or something (she had forgotten that part of the story, because of the impact of what came next) had just come back from Brsadin, where he had been in the same platoon as Lazar. "So what did he say, how is Lazar?" asked Angela, breathlessly, her voice weak with emotion. "He's OK," the person she knew replied, shrugging her shoulders, "I suppose."

Lazar was killed three days later. The news of his death reached us by telephone, in Angela's mother's choking voice. Angela vomited all day long. I didn't go to work so I could be with her. I was afraid for our unborn child. What were we bringing it into (I wondered, holding Angela's brow, clammy with cold sweat), what splendors could we offer it, what could we teach it, and where was that little bit of promised brightness in our existence?

59

How I Fell in Love with Dejan All Over Again

The next morning I awoke weighed down by cowardice and impotence. Unease at the fact that we had nothing left apart from despair, and the fear that like this miserable capital we would not find it easy to remain on our feet, shook me like a fever. Angela was, naturally, far worse. She stepped into the new day, after a sleepless night, with a high temperature and colorless eyes. Not having slept either, I stayed home from work that day as well. Then I showered and ran into town to try to bargain for at least some of the medicines on the list Angela had made for me.

As soon as I stepped out of the dusty hallway into the wet black street, I noticed that something had happened in the course of the night we had spent in senseless conversations about Lazar punctuated by sobs, that night when, for the first time, Angela's tears had seemed to me false, although I had immediately dismissed that heretical thought. As always, as soon as I emerged from Molerova Street onto the Bulevar Revolucije, in the pause between two waves of street din, several curses reached me from different directions. It was the eternal murmur of the dissatisfied, which always sickened me, a sterile whining that was never going to lead anywhere. But this time the murmur had a fresher tone—a discreet but fateful discourse. That crude canonical chant, brutal in its impotence, was enriched by a ghostly, touching phrase—resulting from the participating voices. Eluding my sense of hearing, that phrase irritated me instinctively, and in my light-headed state, all at once I was sorry for all the people in this world for whom there is nothing left but to swear (and I had once mocked them arrogantly). I felt sorry for all of us. In the glare of a sudden and all-pervasive vision that split the ordinary street scene before my eyes, I caught sight of all of us, running, while the ground beneath our feet was breaking up and opening with a terrible cracking sound, and out of those depths came the unbearable stench of the centuries, which, in our inertia, we had failed to use in a dignified way; a great, slimy, pulsating monster was mocking us from in there, unconcerned about the horror we were conjuring up with our irresolute movements, and our desire not to be. In the course of this carnal bacchanalia, which lasted for one second, the chosen victims had vanished randomly into the depths of that well of flesh. There were many of them. All those who had not managed to find a shelter, all those who had been caught unawares, they were all whisked away, like kites snatched from our hands by the November gales.

. . .

I ought, presumably, to have been horrified, but, like many of my fellow citizens, I endeavored to move along the spittle-covered streets, with the practiced step of a native who walks without fear along the foot of a live volcano on the island where his tribe has survived, despite the many victims claimed by the volcano, for generations. I went to a few chemist's shops, until I found three of the seven medicines on the list, concentrating on the job at hand, and when I called Angela from a telephone box to make sure that everything was all right, I got the answering machine. I put the receiver down with a sense of relief. It was a sure sign that Angela had somehow managed to fall asleep. And so, looking around the street, I began to see with my inner eye as well—the selfish eye of personal freedom—glad that I didn't have to rush anywhere, that, in principle, there was nothing stalking me with the intention of devouring me. The street gleamed under the influence of this better understanding, and somewhere on its other side, in the mass of people moving over there, I detected the one-armed Dejan. "Hey!" I shouted, excited at the agreeable logic of the fact that I was meeting him just a day after we had learned of Lazar's death. In truth, the two of them had hardly known each other, but now they belonged, each in his own unhappy way, to the same unregistered club. The step with which Dejan walked was so swift that his right sleeve, gaping open (and loose, because Dejan had not sewn it up, as the disabled usually did, or shoved it into one of his pockets), whipped the passersby who tried to avoid its lash. Afraid of losing him in the throng, I shouted, more loudly than a moment before, "Hey, Dejan! Wait!" He stopped abruptly, as though cut down by a hail of bullets and, strikingly pale, squinted in my direction. Recognizing me, he smiled with relief and waited for me to catch up with him. We shook with our left hands, pretending it was nothing unusual. I was glad to see Dejan smiling, and we set off together for Molerova Street, since I had done what I had to do, and he had some business in the neighborhood. Walking beside me, Dejan bravely did all he could to give the impression that everything was fine, but some sort of change—a change that was, of course, harder to detect than the brutal absence of his right arm—permeated that demanding daylong projection and spoiled it. The first short circuit came when he asked me, casually, it seemed: "How is everyone?" like a student who has just come back from a term abroad, but definitely not like Dejan. His face was twisted with the uncertainty that was stifling him, as he let such an ordinary question pass his lips, cursing inwardly, I imagine, and this transformed the simple unusualness of our situation into a clumsy monster.

Embarrassed, moved, I managed not to reply. Changing the subject absentmindedly, I noticed Dejan's nervous tic. He looked like an animal that has just been caught in a trap. He knew, as I did, that his unfortunate question had opened a crack in a little door to a Dejan quite different from the one I had known before. I squeezed through (who would not have taken the opportunity?) and saw him speaking twice as fast as before, breaking his words up nervously, hardly completing sentences, and constantly touching the rings on his middle and fourth fingers with the thumb of his remaining hand. And he walked, this new Dejan, with a barely noticeable, but still visible, hop.

But soon afterward, Justice allowed me to even the score. I must emphasize that my intention was reasonable, before the words left me, but who is to say that Dejan's hadn't sounded equally splendid in his head? I wanted to put an end to our skirting around it, because although we had been walking together for no more than ten minutes, it was clear that the shadow of Dejan's lost arm was hovering over every topic, and because of this interference on the line, we did not understand each other as well as we had before. I asked him: "So, how's the arm?"

What I had presumably intended to ask was: "How are things *without* the arm?" but I was embarrassed, and the question mocked me in my fear. Although as I stood there, frozen with discomfort, I could only stutter, my lapse warmed Dejan; he coughed and replied, with a slight smile: "Nothing is the same. You know, it isn't good, but it's OK, right. Some people are still the same. I don't know . . . I've learned not to stand crooked," and his body, of its own accord, placed itself in the habitual attitude of a novice-invalid. Although I seemed to myself like a surgeon whose sweat has just been wiped from his eyes by the patient he was operating on, I felt my love for my friend Dejan blossom with full intensity, in the midst of that mournful month of dying.

Since we had already covered a good half of the boulevard, Dejan increased the tempo of relaying to me everything he intended to tell me. And so, barely keeping up with him, I discovered that he was making new plans: he would no longer be involved in music in any way, he was intending to open a dating service. He even invited me to be his ace for unhappy menopausal women, he promised me millions, in passing, if I shaved off my sideburns, but he didn't give me a chance to respond to the offer. He was carried away by a new subject: that Jelena, his former girlfriend, was never at home when he phoned. So he would chat with Viktoria, Jelena's grandmother, who had loved him before, somehow more completely than Jelena herself. I already knew that any comment of mine would be superfluous, that Dejan wouldn't hear it in any case, so I waited calmly for a pause, but then he started up again. In a different voice, he sank into a long, disconnected lament about the fact that since he had come back to Belgrade, his head was full of a pseudo-march he had learned at the front. He maintained that this irritated him more than the lack of his arm. He would wake up in the middle of the night with the song on his lips, and he wasn't sure whether he was lying on his bed in his parents' home, or whether it was all just the multilayered dream of a man exhausted by battles whose back was aching from the sharp stones under the bed in the bivouac, while shells were cracking outside, and in the chaos of an unexpected attack, people he knew were slumping to the ground around him. Whatever he did, poor Dejan, that march kept coming back to torment him. He would sit on a No. 24 bus just to enjoy that trip around a couple of fine Belgrade streets, and it would begin drumming in his head. He would look at the people in the streets and see nothing but units at ease, wild companies of armed citizens, fingernails and teeth. And they all looked suspicious to him. He was more fearful than he had ever been; once he had gone everywhere and hung around with everyone—there had never been a trace of such fear in him.

At that we stopped, outside the flat in Molerova Street. There was a figure from some kind of Hollywood film about a war veteran walking beside me, and this new Dejan intrigued me. It was logical that he should want to continue on his way, alone, along the boulevard. Our hesitation, in the face of the certainty of our parting, was filled by the wailing of a red truck. "Do you know that Lazar is dead?" I said, through the racket. "Who?" asked Dejan, frowning. "Lazar," I explained. "Angela's brother." Dejan shrugged his shoulders, as though he still didn't understand, or didn't care. He licked his lips and shook his head. He wriggled his five fingers in an involuntary nervous tic. But the face I was watching, amazed (because it was the face of a film personality), expressed a kind of wild, growling gaiety. "Are you sure you won't come in for coffee?" I offered, to ease the tension of the moment, certain that Dejan would not accept the invitation. "I think Angela's asleep, but she would like to see you."

He smiled in return, and shook his head. I could not resist hugging him as we parted. I was firmly convinced that we would not soon talk again, let alone meet, and he struck me, despite everything, as courageous. Because he showed no sign of giving up; he felt bad, but he balanced himself with his remaining arm, and it seemed that one day, maybe even quite soon, he would recover his equilibrium, even if it was through a dating business. Dejan accepted that sudden onrush of affection with gentle submission. Something in him rumbled and broke, but I held him long enough for him to embrace me with his whole arm. Although I was prepared for the experience, nevertheless I almost choked with tears when his stump tapped me, impotently, on the shoulder. There was a kind of harmony in that drumming, after all. It was a stump that would have known in no uncertain terms what to do if it were only given the chance to be an arm again. I cared so much about that stump, at that moment, that I would really have liked to kiss it, out of pure friendship, as one kisses people's foreheads, if it had not seemed so inappropriate.

A Relative, and My Total Nosedive, from Which I Would Emerge in One Piece, Endowed with a Unique Moral

Lazar's body, with its seven bullet holes, arrived in an unusual coffin, accompanied by an escort in regulation brown. The pay, which that body had not managed to receive, was transferred, through the regular channels, to its father's account. Bent over the coffin, Mihailo wept. The young lieutenant from the escort did not know what to say; it was clear that the whole situation maddened him. "You must be strong," he kept repeating in a monotonous voice.

Of Lazar's friends, despite the announcement in

the papers giving information about the time and place of the cremation, there was neither sight nor sound. They sat in their Temple, unconcerned about the outer world, which, unenlightened, was subject to blows without a shield such as theirs. They either just sat, sunk in the quality tonic of their own dogma, or else, to do them justice, maybe they did somehow mourn Lazar, but had decided not to share their grief with us. Generally speaking, the absence of young people at the cemetery was disappointing. Apart from the two soldiers, who had to be there, and one of Lazar and Angela's distant relatives, the shambling procession was made up of middle-aged people in dark coats, and several antique noses blue with cold. In that procession, I felt like an intruder, remote from Angela, who was protected by her position at the head of the procession, her black clothes, the previously mentioned pallor in her eyes that remained until the birth of our child, and her undeniable stomach. I walked, therefore, with an uncertain step, forcibly removed from my mainstay. In order to understand my participation in the unusual adventure that grew out of this, the reader must realize that I wasn't having an easy time!

I have already mentioned that in the course of the last few years of my life, I had seen many funerals, but I had not participated in anything like this. The sorrowful and comic ritual, involuntarily arranged, was entirely in keeping with my personal notion of Lazar, and after the whole madness came to an end, at the moment when I sank into a relaxing sleep, Lazar shone before me with the halo of a saint. If one overlooks the hearty slap administered by a priest to a novice at the entrance to the cemetery just as we were assembling, one could say that everything had a restrained dignity, up until the moment when the funeral official with thick glasses (I had seen him at earlier cremations), carrying out his discreet arrangements, went to give the sign to his invisible colleague that the coffin containing Lazar's body could be lowered into the depths of purgatory by activating a simple hydraulic lever. Taking a ritual step backward, he waved energetically like a traffic policeman, then bumped into a rubber plant and toppled onto the marble floor, his behind slapping loudly against it. "Ouch!" he cried, on top of everything. The relative I have already mentioned, who was standing beside me, could not contain herself. She laughed, and her giggle resounded oddly in that place where people so rarely laugh. As she froze in the face of the poisonous glances of the majority of those present, the organizer recovered from his shock. The coffin disappeared, creaking, into the depths of the crematorium, and it seemed as though, at any moment, the worn-out cable would snap and the coffin would hit the ground and shatter into pieces. I was so overcome by panic at that possibility that I had to slip outside, to get some air. As I tiptoed out, a renewed burst of giggles reached my ears, followed by the clattering of a woman's high-heeled shoes. Then I felt very clearly the heat of her glance on my back; I had reached the entrance, the fresh air relieved me, and a scene stretched before me that would have been idyllic had the circumstances only been different: six frozen workmen in jerkins were huddled around an abandoned silver tray with the traditional Orthodox funeral dish of sweet wheat and brandy, helping themselves straight from the bottle. I turned on my heels to confront the eyes that had followed me, and a clanging of little spring bells, unseemly at that time of year, tickled the hairs on the inner side of my thigh.

"I don't know what came over me," said the Relative in a soft, melodious voice, with a serious expression. She had eyes as black as pitch, and her full, smooth lips made her romantically beautiful. She spoke without any kind of accent, very calmly, but she bore her divinity in a quite different way from Angela. Angela dwelt in her beauty with her whole being, like the proprietor of a magnificent garment. The Relative bore her own beauty under lock and key, she trembled with fiery shame and amazingly obvious expectations, and I trembled before her, as I might have done in the company of a film star appearing before me in a favorite role, although she was in fact only an ordinary good-looking girl, like many others in Belgrade.

Exchanging a few incidental sentences, we walked along the cemetery path, one of those little walkways lined with crosses that meander unpredictably in front of you. We stepped slowly. Almost imperceptibly, the Relative bestowed on me her warm, dry hand. As if in a crackly black and white film, snow began to fall. I remembered a recent film with Dejan in the leading role that was certainly in color, but was nevertheless pale in comparison with this. The large flakes were falling on our faces; leaning against the cracked canvas with the panorama of the old cemetery, according to the code of an East European dream, I broke all the rules—I kissed her. She slipped her hand under my coat, and when she squeezed what she found there, I gasped with pleasure, and pain. In return, I bit her ear. Her earring was deliciously cold. Everything that was happening represented such a fulfillment of my sexual fantasies—entwining with a stranger whose name I did not even know, according to an agreement made without words, by some other form of understanding—that, excited as I was, I could only breathe heavily, endeavoring to suppress to whatever degree possible all the awkwardness of this supremely unseemly situation. I want to say that I tried to enjoy the role that had been assigned to me. And it was only when I had come into the dish of the Relative's palm that I noticed the pimples on her cheeks, and I was overcome with shame. I pinched and caught myself as I did up my fly. She smiled, and kissed me on the neck. "Have you got a cigarette?" she asked me tenderly. My underpants were full of snowflakes. "No," I replied. "Have you got a handkerchief?" She smiled again, mocking me. "No," she answered, imitating the way I had pronounced the same word a moment before. "But I'll bring one next time." I hurried to fix my clothes while the Relative, straightening her hair with her other hand, slowly wiped the palm of her right hand on the cold surface of a nearby cross. This left her with a sticky black dusty stain on her hand. "Are you a student?" I said then, quite stupidly and superfluously. Hunching my shoulders in shame, I was left without an answer, as I deserved. To make things as black as they could be, hurrying to join the grieving group, and at the same time trying to leave the Relative behind me, I stepped up to my knees in mud.

I had never done anything of the kind before. I had never *betrayed* Angela, as the inadequate expression goes. Not that I would have had anything against it, it's just that the coefficient of tactics, effort, and deceit demanded by *betrayal* always seemed too great. I never had the patience for such total manipulation. But I used to do those things for myself, especially when everything got to be too much for me. Once it was done, nothing was any easier, but, in addition to the semen fluid, an inner tension flowed out of me, and that brought me some moments of respite, until the pressure built up again. I think that the event I have described sprang from such a need. After it, despite a certain shame for what I had done—caused, in truth, more by superstition than by marital guilt—I didn't actually feel any more guilty than I would have if I had gone off by myself to relieve myself behind a cross. Although I have to say that I was terrified that Angela would notice something. As soon as I joined the little group hovering in the open space by the cemetery gate, evidently waiting for me, with the Relative who was walking a dozen paces behind me, indisputable on the broad path, my gaze met the two cold, swollen eyes of my wife. I joined her and, with a dignified expression, quietly confided a great secret to her: "She asked me to go for a walk with her; she didn't feel well . . ." And who knows? Maybe Angela believed me. However, something was threatening me from above, something in the face of which lies are no use. An invisible finger pointed straight at me. But everything soon calmed down. No lightning appeared from the clouds to punish me for blasphemy, for violating the holy vows of matrimony, and the sociopathological absence of any kind of moral responsibility. Here, at the very gate of the cemetery, strengthened by Angela's dull expression, I smiled at the absolute impotence of the heavens: So, it's true! Everything is possible.

About My Mother and Father

In order to attend the funeral, my parents had arrived some days earlier from the village of K. in Fruška Gora. Knowing their firm principles and their general unwillingness to alter arrangements that had been made in advance, I took that gesture as a sign of sincere grief for Lazar, of whom they too had been particularly fond during his lifetime.

As it does for many people who have spent their lives in the city, the village represented for my father and mother a source of exotic pleasures. For that reason, as soon as they had both retired, they set off to spend the greater part of the year there, and to imitate faithfully the village way of life. Holding out for maximum authenticity, they decided not to supply electricity to the outside toilet situated at the end of a steep courtyard, so if they absolutely had to get up during the night, they made their way bravely into that malodorous darkness, black as ink, into that meeting place of spiders and blowflies—otherwise they held on. But I understood why they liked living in K. My grandmother's house was a real masterpiece of secular architecture, shaped by a shortage or superfluity of particular materials (the house was built during 1947 and 1948), by the inadequate professional knowledge and profound nostalgia of the builders (they were German prisoners-of-war captured in Yugoslavia who were, unexpectedly, deported back to Germany without completing their work), and, above all, by the organizational caprices of my grandmother, whose carping outbursts terrified the German builders. One may assume that in that throng of different craftsmen there did exist some kind of architect who had conceived the house, in its basic lines, but he had been quick to exchange his original ideas for peaceful coexistence with his short-tempered taskmaster, because he had obviously adopted and carried out all my grandmother's wishes, however illogical, without hesitation, even as he tried, as far as it was possible, to leave his personal stamp on the architecture of the house. That is how that building came into being with its tiled, pyramidal roof (made not of unbaked brick, as one might have expected, since there was always plenty of mud and straw about, but of expertly selected stone pieces predominantly blue and yellow in tone, at Grandmother's insistence), and with windows framed with charmingly arranged bricks, according to the craftsmen's own instinct. Here, in tubs made of wooden lemon crates, my mother grew the most varied flowers, and if the posited designer, should he ever have existed and should he still have been alive, had happened to appear in the village of K. to inspect his distant work, he would have been agreeably surprised to note how well and harmoniously that eclectic building of his had settled into the very edge of a slope, and with what love its present owners tended and maintained it. My mother decorated the house with flowers of all conceivable colors, and, thanks to my father, the unfinished side of the house that faced the backyard was covered in vines. Here, in the hollows, sparrows built their nests, and my father was sometimes obliged to chase them away with an air gun in his hand, while they flew at rooftop level, avoiding his marksman's skill, deriding him.

The local people had not yet forgotten the German builders when new workmen arrived in the village, led by a state artist in uniform. And soon, on one of the neighboring hills, a monument to a Warrior was erected, and emblazoned across his stomach—according to the artist's ingenious plan—were the names of all the victims from the village of K. who had fallen in the struggle against the occupier and local traitors. Among them was the name of my paternal grandfather, although he had never fought against anyone. He had lived in the village as a teacher. He had produced an illegitimate child with my grandmother—my father. He once grew a mustache and shaved it off a few months later. He had planned to take up beekeeping, but was thwarted: he was shot, for no apparent reason.

High above the flat head of the Warrior, the sky

had been churning up westerly or easterly clouds, undis-turbed until recently. At the time of the events in this book, insofar as anyone felt inclined to sit on the bench in front of the crumbling village church, the baroque façade of which had been slowly atrophying since 1764, and which was soon to be restored under the direction of a young, ambitious priest, it was possible—despite the high-frequency screeching of the shopkeeper's transistor—to hear, all day long, to one's heart's content, the muffled thunder of gunfire on the other side of the hill.

The majority of the male population of K. had been mobilized. Those who were left (for the most part, old men, the village drunks, and wastrels) enjoyed regular afternoon gatherings in the center of the village, under the arch or in front of the shop, depending on their taste. My father had grown close to them, and as a retired high-ranking officer, he enjoyed his honored status as their main spokesman. Although the company usually chewed over some theme that was more or less obscure to everyone, when my father was in a good mood, he would open the portals straight into his soldier-cum-high-school-teacher's past, settle all their uncertainties with wafers of logistics and strategy, explaining to the fascinated company the advantages of particular types of weapons over others, but as to the real questions—such as why there were no young men in the village and who was going to work the land when the time came for it—my father would keep those, more personal pronouncements haughtily to himself. When eventually he felt he had said all he had to say, he would make his excuses and leave them. I see him walking with an easy step, potbellied, with gray hair and strong teeth, greeting people to the left and right, like the father I remember from the time when he used to beat our neighbor, his colleague from the Higher Military Academy, at chess every day, before lunch. Lieutenant Colonel Kreft had moved out of Belgrade back to Slovenia that summer, and I suppose my father missed that bit of bragging. If all of this bored him, he knew, although he did not make such decisions easily, that with my mother's help, he could always pack up his things and they could be back in Belgrade in an hour. They would leave the house and garden, and the *chardak* (in the standard Srem region design), as well as the pigsty that was not used for anything, in the charge of a one-eyed male cat with a broken jaw that had, as Mother enjoyed saying, "adopted them."

My parents had met Lazar only a couple of times, but they loved him madly, without cause, and I found that love all the more unusual in that I could never quite gauge whether they loved me, their only child, at all. Suppressing their personal pain, sensitive to the hierarchy that reigns among the bereaved, they were evidently determined not to stand out in any way at the funeral. However, my mother did not know how to avoid getting irritated—irritation being for her a good substitute for all conflicting emotions. Still, she avoided too hasty reactions. So, when my father took out a cigarette and lighter in the chapel, intending to smoke, she had simply pinched him in the thigh, looking coldly in the opposite direction. He leapt aside in astonishment and pain, but he got the message, and the incident passed unnoticed. They spent the rest of the ceremony at the head of the procession, they talked in whispers, but only if they had to, and their faces expressed faultless grief, and dignity. And at the funeral feast, where, at a late hour, all the grief was suddenly transformed into an ugly parody of grief, my parents and the other guests, following a strange impulse, began singing an old song about unhappy love, faded roses, and snow.

I expected them to leave Belgrade the following day, so my surprise was enormous when that morning, at the door of our flat in Molerova Street, there appeared, of all people in the world, my father. This man who hardly knew us was standing in front of us smiling, with his French cap pulled down over his eyes.

I would not have been so surprised had my mother appeared, but my father had politely stepped aside throughout my childhood, leaving me alone in the open spaces of all the crucial situations by simply disappearing around the corner, so that I never succeeded in grasping whether, in this long-drawn-out game, the two of us were partners or opponents. Sometimes, of course, I would feel the spotlight of his attention directed at me, and I would be glad of its warm ray, but those moments were so rare that there was no alternative but for me to make a fetish of them as long as they lasted, for those upsurges of fatherly inspiration appeared according to some mysterious logic of their own, and disappeared in the same way. After that, once again cool, the two of us would revert to our established roles as strangers who would greet each other warmly if they happened to meet on the same side of the street, but preferred not to meet at all.

And then, suddenly (after several years during which we saw each other at intervals of between six and a whole seventeen months), my father was here: he put his beret and scarf down in the hall. He was curious to see the flat, and I could not figure out what effect Angela's aggressive concept of organizing her living space, crammed with flowers, heavy drapes, dusty photographs, and mirrors, had on him, but, if nothing else, the kitchen must surely have impressed him by its size. His sincere delight in it all annoyed me. "But you bought me the flat," I reminded him, and not to get involved in a disagreeable subject, he rubbed his hands enthusiastically and said: "I'm really hungry. What about you two?"

81

That was how my father usurped our kitchen, evidently determined to make himself at home. He arrived every day with baskets of food and made us meals. "Are your folks splitting up?" whispered Angela with an anxious expression, during his third visit; he appeared in the living room a second later carrying a tray with a frying pan piled high with a glorious ham-and-cheese omelette. He came in like that, with a triumphant step, holding a Jena-glass dish in which crispy pancakes filled with cheese, fried bacon, cream, and eggs were still sizzling. Sometimes he served us simply, toast rubbed with garlic and spread with butter, and he regularly drank tea (we preferred black coffee), with quite a lot of rum and sugar. I don't remember whether he used to drink it like that when we were living in the same house, but now that drink, with its intoxicating aroma, obviously cheered him.

With time his visits acquired the protection of Habit. I was determinedly avoiding going to work, declaring myself ill over the telephone, so as to be present as long as my father's visits lasted. In the course of several initial meetings, they radiated Meaning, and it was great for us because we knew exactly when my father would come, what he would do when he was with us, how long he'd be able to hold out, and why he would leave us. And once he had left, we had virtually the whole day in front of us. My father's visits didn't disturb anything. We could do absolutely anything in his presence, and whatever we did was greeted with unmistakable signs of approval. And then it dawned on us! Why, my father was here to make our life agreeable! In that filial euphoria, it occurred to me that Lazar's death, as far as I personally was concerned, was not such a bad investment in view of my father's transformation, but even in that ecstatic state I was sufficiently cautious to add (just in case): on condition that it was for good, which, of course, it couldn't be.

On the other hand, we shouldn't exaggerate. Sometimes he got on our nerves. If he bent down to pick something up from the floor (and he kept dropping things), his left knee would generally slip out of its socket, and he would be obliged to put it back into place, with a nauseating clicking of the bones and a spasm in his vein-lined face. Despite the fact that Angela tried to be maximally pleasant to him, once, unable to hold it in, she shrieked, "Oh, go to the doctor, for god's sake!"—at which my father, with an innocent expression, asked, "What for?" That was his great sense of humor. After several people had made similar remarks, and since he had no intention of visiting a doctor, because he despised them, he concluded that it would be simplest for him to build a firm defensive wall around himself. And so, if Angela were to respond, "What do you mean 'what for'? Go and see a doctor about that knee of yours, it's appalling!" he would simply exhale.

He would not be angry with Angela even if, by some chance, she swore at him. He tolerated her fury: he interpreted it as the frustration of a novice that would soon pass, and then Angela would stop paying attention to his knee, just like me and my mother, my father's brother, and Franc Kreft, our erstwhile neighbor.

The cooling factor was the realization that from the first day, my father was obviously here on account of Angela; he hardly noticed me. I would have liked to be able to interpret that as an offer of help, because Angela really did need some kind of help, but he was involved in a more complex mission. For all his stiffness, he was intending to become Angela's sincere friend. Everything was subordinated to that holy aim, even the occasional short circuit that would occur between them, like the business with the knee. The process of their growing close developed smoothly, and I began to understand that, in an indirect way, it did include me as well. This new rootedness appealed to me, it made breathing easier. I also experienced something new: I saw the layers of protective skin fall away from my father. "How was your visit to the gynecologist?" he would ask, his eyebrows twitching anxiously, after Angela returned from a checkup. And when she confirmed that everything was in perfect order, he murmured, "I never imagined such a thing: a grandchild . . ." Our conversations exuded a pleasant calm, and when my father sighed and sang, "Oh, children, children," we would know that he wasn't going to say anything more. Getting up, he reached for his beret, I helped him put on his coat, we both saw him to the door. Angela waddled behind me, in her comical body, but with an angelic expression. With one foot in the hall, he would wave to us with a gesture that was unusually shy. Every time, I would ask myself whether it was possible that a father could be so diffident.

Although it lasted only for perhaps ten days, his transformation intrigued me. Never in my wildest dreams did I expect such an eruption of good will from my mother. My mother was a cold, if close, constant presence, keeping always the same agreeable distance from me. And although not a day passed without our speaking on the telephone, and we had her over twice, albeit in the evening, which my mother considered the only possible time for visits, her principled nonappearances with my father indicated that she was maintaining her established position through her conscious will. Nevertheless, I managed to detect in her, too, an extremely unusual change, only on a quite different level. It emerged that my mother belonged to a whole class of intellectuals who proved capable only of the inadmissible naïveté of a child. I'm not complaining, but I did expect more of my mother. I have the right to that express demand, and to disappointment in the dominant being in my life.

So it happened, a little sadly, that my father surprised me agreeably, but that my mother disappointed me a bit. For the first time, I understood him better, but not her. And I was living through the thirtieth year of my life. Perhaps that had something to do with my afternoon rest. I don't know.

Because, in truth, nothing happened. Only this: when she was asked, at the funeral feast, how she withstood the firing they were obliged to bear night after night in the country, because the front line was so close, my mother lit a cigarette, and only then, swathed in bluish smoke, did she turn to her companion, with an apologetic smile. "It's dreadful, you know," she said, "but it's a fact: you get used to everything."

PART III

December 1991

Everything Is Slowing Down, Even the Clocks Seem to Tick More Slowly—About the Ideal Drafter—The Trading Company "Grotteske Kid" Inc.—Memories from a Child's Room—With Vanja About This and That, Including Dejan—In the Hold

Everything Is Slowing Down, Even the Clocks Seem to Tick More Slowly

I close my eyes under the orange down quilt, right up against Angela's body, which has just buttoned itself into sleep, and Lazar is embodied in a flaming chamber: he jumps out of a truck somewhere in Brsadin, which is a knot of Renaissance streets. The spiral lanes bear the clatter of his metal-tipped soles over the cobbles; his pigtail flutters freely, growing into a mane, then a whip. Knocking against the façades of the ancient houses with first-floor balconies, pieces of plaster fall away from them and crash to the ground. All the streets of this Renaissance town pour into the square, in the center of which, as at its navel, rises a coliseum. Lazar, followed by his pigtail, which has reached unimaginable dimensions, arrives at the main entrance, above which gleams the inscription ENTRANCE. The entrance is guarded by armed types in tight uniforms, and although their expressions are generally scowling, they register a benign attitude to Lazar's appearance and greet him with a polite bow. Running past them, Lazar finally arrives on the other side, with his feet on a dusty podium. Here, listening to the reaction of the masses, he will stop. And he can stand like this for hours, exposed to the gaze of the crowd—nothing more will happen. The orange quilt does not reveal the dream's punch line.

Or else I dream of a child tearing itself out of its mother's arms in order to fly to the peacetime Lazar, and biting a piece of flesh out of his thigh with its sharp little teeth. While Lazar doubles over in pain, the child returns to the security of its mother's embrace. Without suggesting, by her gesture, that anything out of the ordinary has occurred, she carefully removes from its mouth a piece of saffron-colored material.

On another occasion I close my eyes under the orange down quilt and Angela is feeling my pulse, staring into my pupils, and then confiding to someone next to her: "I think he's dead now." Then she vanishes, and a rubber hand with a razor blade dramatically enters my field of vision and lowers itself toward the crown of my head. As it cuts into my skin, I feel no pain, but I experience that action, which I cannot see, abstractly. Out of my head, as from a burst marrow, pour seeds, and a kind of mucus, but sweet—like lime tea sweetened with honey. The images jostle a bit before my eyes, and then I am obliged to look at Angela. Her legs apart, naked, she has been secured to a chrome-plated neo-inquisitorial torture device. She is unable to do anything other than lie there and moan. Nine masked doctors in togas take out of her a sex-less plastic doll. When it is turned on its belly, the doll flutters its lifeless eyelids and says: "Mama." Without taking the binding from his head, the chief doctor declares, "It had begun to fester. In a couple of hours we would have had to intervene in the uterus. You understand, we had no choice."

I decided that if I got involved in any such horrors again, I would suggest to Angela that we change the bedclothes. Nevertheless, I was glad that I could sleep at all. Waking up in the very gullet of the gloomy winter morning would have been more painful than the most painful dreams. That was why, after my parents had left Belgrade again and we were deprived of the pleasure of my father's daily visits, and calculating that Angela's time must be near, I telephoned to transform that unjustified sick leave into an annual holiday. Maybe I should have done so face-to-face. As it was, my behavior resembled the maneuvering of someone preparing to give notice, and it could easily have happened—as it did happen, although a little later—that the boss would wish to hurry me so that he could remove me from the payroll on his own initiative, but I did not, quite simply, have the strength to confront him. Apart from that, what I despised above all was the muddy bus ride as far as Banovo Brdo. And I discovered that even the possibility of dismissal did not alarm me unduly. So what? I reflected, puffing myself up with defiance. I'll find a better job, in any case.

Angela and I spent the first days of December sleeping until noon, or later, after which we would usually stagger off somewhere for coffee and croissants. Then we would go to Kalemegdan Park or visit someone. We spent our few reserves of cash exclusively on insignificant trifles. In the evening, friends would come by and we would sit around until the early hours or the first morning buses. Only Angela would take herself off to bed before midnight, or she would choose to stay and sleep among us, on a heap of coats. It turned out that Lazar's death had ushered in a peace we had lacked before. The funeral and the events that followed it had brought about a collective reconciliation. Even relations between Angela and her parents lightened. Lazar emerged as the only casualty of these otherwise positive developments. The impossibility of communication, of participation in our affairs, pushed him out of our everyday life, and he could not have been pleased, watching from on high as those closest to him concerned themselves with earthly problems, not displaying the slightest will to investigate his case, and to see what had happened to him there, in Brsadin, during the eleven days of his heroic warfaring. Although it is unrewarding to express a judgment on certain matters, as far as his concrete case was concerned, I am ready to maintain, in defense of those of us who have remained alive, that even before his unfortunate death, Lazar existed for his family largely in the form of a locked bathroom door. Shifting from one foot to the other in the corridor, the rest of the household had only one consolation. "He's meditating," they would agree, and they would go off to shift from foot to foot and suffer someplace where they wouldn't disturb him. Only Angela, while she still lived in that house, and as ever insistent on her rights, would beat her fists furiously on the door for ten minutes on end, demanding that Lazar stop his "mantraing." Then Vida and Mihailo would tremble and pace up and down nervously in a far corner of the flat. They would prefer to pee at a neighbor's place rather than risk behaving like Angela. Not for anything in the world would they allow Lazar to punish them again by refusing food for several days at a time, by frequently locking himself in his room, by the black rings under his eyes and the sadly withered cheeks of a born ascetic—sadistic punishments that, in keeping with his deadly consistency, could last for several weeks.

Angela, whose gynecologist had predicted a strong, healthy child, liked to feel that Lazar had gone off on the wings of Will and Reason, rather than that he had been abducted. I believed that she was right. Everything that had happened was perfectly in keeping with a logical epilogue to his mission on this earth. Regardless of her conviction, however, Angela sometimes wept bitterly. I repented for ever having doubted her tears. She could think whatever she liked, I hummed to myself, full of compassionate love; she was the only one of us who would never get over Lazar's death.

Nevertheless, despite all those tears (which were, after all, tears of consolation, not of pain), everything around us was closing in. Everything was slowing down, even the clocks seemed to tick more slowly. And if, in those first days of December, we were living through a romanticized version of our lives, who could have blamed us? Too many things had broken over our backs for us to be tormented by any day-to-day traumas, such as all that jostling on buses, all those goings to work and sweaty comings home, where Angela would already be tired and irritable with loneliness, and the hour-long telephone conversations with which she filled her days. That was why we enjoyed an absence of obligations. We knew that in just a couple of weeks, a new life quite different from this one was in store for us—a life like a hectic clock, with a small being who still made itself known only with pulses and sounds from Angela's stomach. Until that day came, we had decided to rest. We would have liked to spend all our money on drugs—but were restrained, as we had been for the last nine months, by Angela's pregnancy.

95

About the Ideal Drafter

In that atypical state of calm, insofar as there was anything I feared, it was the drafters. Once they knocked for a long time on our next-door neighbor's door. Eventually his father answered. When he told them that his son was not there, that he had not been living there for a long time, that he did not know his current address, that they should not take his word for it but he thought maybe he was abroad, it was perfectly clear that he was lying. He was an honest man who was not accustomed to lying. But, nevertheless, he showed more loyalty to his son than Lazar's parents, and refused to accept the draft paper. The drafters sniggered. There were two of them: one wore jeans and a long coat, the other was in the uniform of the Yugoslav People's Army. That one had long blond hair and smooth cheeks, but still, he behaved like a hooligan. He spat on the ground so often that in the course of the few minutes they spent on our floor, he showered the entire available space, and then he started to shift his weight from one foot to the other, in a nervous tic. When they finally resolved to leave the unfortunate, sweating father in peace, the Blond slid down the banisters to the floor below. Before that, to my horror, he had peered through the peephole in my door, which had enabled me to observe them unhindered, as though he knew that I was on the other side, watching and fearful. That sudden movement of his shook me. His face began to stretch, it looked as though he were going to pour himself entirely into his own nose and then explode, but his friend called him away, pulling at the sleeve of his regulation brown windbreaker.

That increased my fear, spicing it with tingling excitement. Whenever I imagined the drafter at my own door, he was what I saw. In my imagination, he represented the blond-haired god of all the hooligans. With him at our head, Ivan and Dejan and Lazar and I, and another ten thousand times the four of us, filled the main roads, seized the mountain passes, swam across the rivers of confrontation, trod down fields of corn; rocks cracked beneath our feet, we rushed headlong into seas, our faces splitting their impregnated blue surface. Brides awaited us in the depths, with seaweed in their hair. As we marched, we were equipped with catapults, water pistols, and little bottles of invisible ink. Above our heads flew kites and paper aeroplanes. Toward us, in identical columns, came Tomislav and Sven and Marin and Ivica.* If we met, we would discover what sort of weapons they had.

*Typical Croatian men's names.—TRANS.

97

The Trading Company "Grotteske Kid" Inc.

It was at that time that I also realized Dejan had no intention of establishing his personal civilian balance through a dating service. My evidence was a parcel sent to our address containing two beautifully designed boxes, on which, in shrieking letters, was written GROTTESKE!, along with a letter in a separate envelope. In the first of the boxes was a child's red T-shirt, over the entire surface of which was written, in yellow letters, N R G. There was the same inscription, only smaller, on each of the sleeves. The other T-shirt was similar to the first, except that the background was green, the letters white, and they read: EMICKY EMUSO. That the parcel came from Dejan, we gathered (although the reader knows already) only at the end of the whole inspection, when we opened the envelope with the mysterious label: T.C. "GROTTESKE KID" INC. The sender, revealed as Dejan, wrote:

> As I have given up the idea of the business I intended to involve you in, I was afraid of forgetting you too soon, so I dreamed up this business, which will have lots to do with you. I myself designed the T-shirts I am sending you, and I've found excellent

manufacturers, as you can see from these samples. This is just a fragment of my children's collection, and all the prototypes, so to speak, will be made by the same people. As far as your involvement goes, my idea is that you should use these samples to convince your boss that we should go into business, because I know you're in the wholesale textile and clothing market. I would offer them at the following rates, which I believe are exceptionally favorable, [etc., etc.]

"I knew it!" I shouted with pure delight, waving the letter in front of Angela's nose. What I knew, in fact, was that Dejan was the only normal person in this part of the world. "Of course, man!" I called out to him that I would go along with everything, aware that he couldn't hear me through the window. Angela wisely ignored me. She looked at the T-shirts with interest, inside and out, critical of the seams (she maintained they were amateurish), but still she wanted to be sure: "Are these samples ours to keep?"

I was paternally proud of Dejan's commercial hyperactivity. The T-shirts were great, there was nothing wrong with the seams, and I resolved to interrupt my annual leave to engage my boss on their behalf in good time. At the same time, I prepared to answer Dejan with an equally businesslike letter, in which I would inform him that this was not a good time of year for commerce, as it was nearly the New Year, and everything was tied up, and new deals would not be made until the end of January, but, nevertheless, it was good to start now, so that the whole process of buying and selling should get going in good time. I also intended to suggest that he send us a formal estimate of how many different T-shirts he could produce by then, with diagrams and approximate figures. I particularly wanted to contribute to the realization of the first income in Dejan's life. In this seething maw of a city, where so many fell by the wayside because they lacked the proper weapons for the battle against dissatisfaction, surrounded by fellow citizens who knew only how to raise their hands in pained surprise at the injustice that oppressed us, Dejan had risen up with all the Socialist Realist splendor of the Worker. Other people's lives were falling apart under the prevailing pressure. They had appeared happy and secure, and then people they were fond of started to abandon them, they discovered that their wives were cheating on them with their best friends, husbands began beating them with signet rings for some reason, they were getting poorer by the day, but Dejan, handicapped as he was, was in the mood for big business! Meanwhile, they had given up smoking, for months they had not bought anything more substantial than a pair of socks, they used to eat in restaurants but now were more and more often to be seen breaking eggs over a burned frying pan, while ham and the most ordinary mousetrap cheese had become a kind of luxury. To be fair, gazing into the gloomy distance, they were still well-off, *as long as things stayed like this*. They were preparing themselves for the time when poverty *really* hit them, and they would stop eating altogether. They were discovering that they were capable of sinking deeper than they could have imagined, and they were interested in testing their attitude to suffering. They summoned the strength for such easy surrender from the specific satisfaction of the pragmatist under the whip, who, after the fiftieth of a hundred blows, says: "Objectively, I could withstand the same again!"

In a way, I would be flattering myself if I distinguished myself from this miserable herd, and that made me all the more pleased for Dejan, who was keeping his head above water in this land of drowning people, kicking energetically, determined to win. Transformed into a charismatic figure from a sentimental Hollywood fairy tale about a war veteran, he had dragged himself through hell and paid the price, without being compensated by so much as a philosophical moral, for there was no moral to be drawn in this hell. But still, he had not returned as an empty shell. Obliged to look upon his set of drums as a useless gadget that took up half his room, he sold it without hesitation and set off in search of a new kind of activity. From his clumsy dating service idea, he had quickly reached a firmer footing. His T-shirts were brilliant.

I want to stress that I had never prostrated myself before Dejan. But since our November meeting I had begun to adore him, and I accepted the T-shirts, gratified that my outpourings of infinite trust and love had not been misplaced. All I could do was admire him with adolescent tenacity, but I should have known it was unhealthy to nurture such emotions. That evening I talked about him at such length and with such exaltation that in the end Angela was offended, and she spent the whole night firmly pressed into her side of the bed. The next morning she turned to me, at breakfast, and said, munching a bun from the nearby bakery, "Listen, if Dejan's so fantastic, why don't you live together?" But then she smiled, right away. I think Dejan interested her as well, in a particular way. As a man, he was perfect, and Angela was exceptionally susceptible to handsome men. There was nothing that Angela was not capable of forgiving a handsome man. According to her, they had a perfect right to behave irresponsibly, even to lose part of their body—my wife was full of understanding for all their whims. She admired women as well, in a way only women can, particularly models with perfect legs, but it was quite clear in her case (though many women won't actually say so) that, aesthetically, men meant more to her. Since I admitted the same feeling for women—their beauty always enchanted me—I understood her, glad that my reaction was not jealousy, which is an underhanded weapon. So it happened that, since she still had not had a chance to see Dejan without his arm and was sufficiently relaxed to show how intrigued she was, Angela asked, "How does it suit him?"

Conscious myself of Dejan's new sex appeal, I replied, "It suits him like Moshe Dayan's black patch."

Memories from a Child's Room

I did not send the intended business letter, however. The very next day I was thrown off course by a sudden initiative of Angela's provoked by her anxiety in the face of her impending delivery, and I submerged myself completely in detailed preparations for the long period of parenthood that was rising up before us, plastically symbolized by the incredible dimensions of Angela's stomach. At the height of that activity, it happened, as before some long journey, that my throat became constricted. And I coughed and growled, while Angela was increasingly bathed in sweat. She packed her things for the hospital, spent ages trying to decide on her choice of underwear, went to her last ultrasound, and then everything was decided; all that was left was for us to await the moment of decision, the warning drumming from her depths, the stretching of the unnamed being in the waters, and—movement.

As I said, I didn't waste time either. While she was doing what she had to do, I assembled the crib in the corner of the bedroom. Above it, on the side wall, I put up a shelf for toys. I placed the few little garments, furry rabbits, and diapers tidily in a drawer. I arranged the talc, reserves of cream, baby's bath foam, diaper rash ointment, and a dozen child's soaps on the side of the bath. Our whole flat already smelled agreeably of children.

When the time came (I repeated to myself feverishly, polishing the furniture in the hall), we would buy plantex-tea, an herbal mixture for stomach cramps with caraway and chamomile, and gripe water. And I threw myself into sterilizing all our little bottles, and all those different kinds of nipple, as well as the blue-and-white thermos for the bottle, in the electric sterilizer. And all that time, which I spent working in different parts of the flat, I kept inventing reasons to stop so that I could slip once again into the bedroom, to press my nose into the toy that smelled of rusks, to turn on the bedside lamp that changed into three playing puppies when lit, to wind up the musical box in the shape of a smiling tomato, because I wanted it to play to me, and to move its naïve eyes to the left and right. I would touch the mobile hanging over the crib to set it in motion, and after a moment's hesitation, it would start moving. Blue-eyed bees circled in an orderly way around a crescent moon in a nightcap. A gigantic frog observed my every movement from the half-light in the corner. Left simply to endure the dust, it had folded its limbs under its great stomach and looked irascible, like an offended Buddha. The only thing that jarred was the yellow of its belly, and its multicolored back, made of rags. A jester in a porkpie hat flew out of a box toward my nose, with a hysterical squeak, darting a shiny red plastic tongue in and out. A teddy bear in an old-fashioned pilot's uniform of brown leather, with a fur collar, and a leather hat with earflaps, was content to observe, through mauve swimming goggles, that tame world of which I too was an inhabitant. I went up to it, to touch it once more, and discovered behind it, not without surprise (although I had personally put each of the toys in its place), a white rabbit with a blue ribbon, and a blue rabbit with a tousled, striped tail. I was particularly fond of the three generations of dolls, which I had placed just there. They were real old-fashioned dolls for little girls dressed in lacy pajamas with their hair tidily drawn into long nightcaps. Our unborn son had been sent them by mistake by some distant, and fairly senile, relative on my mother's side. But despite the obvious error, I did not have the heart to disdain them, I found them so interesting, seated, one in front of the other, in the laps of one another's widespread legs. It was probably because, from the first moment, they had looked to me unbelievably lascivious. Other than in that mad pose, they could not sit properly.

With Vanja About This and That, Including Dejan

However, as soon as that prebirth euphoria was over, my thoughts turned, once again, eagerly, to Dejan. I felt guilty for having abandoned him for so long. Conscious of the belatedness of my reaction, and being familiar with Dejan's innate impatience, I had firmly resolved to give myself a kind of test of my business acumen. On tenterhooks, I decided nevertheless that I would not contact him until I had in my hand a draft contract for the sale of his T-shirts on the basis of the samples he had sent me. I was pleased at the thought of giving him pleasure just when he would have abandoned the idea of cooperation with me, or at least begun to doubt the efficacy of the postal service. The thought of the satisfaction I would give him delighted me, but my decision also had another element that was particularly important to me personally: for the first time in my working life, I had decided to be disloyal to the firm that employed me. Besides, what do I care? I thought. Even if the thing with Dejan was a real commercial hit, I would be unlikely to be rewarded with anything more significant than a standard, miserably average, salary! This way, by helping Dejan, I would be helping myself as well.

Impatient to finally get involved in the process of promoting myself by representing Dejan's children's T-shirts, that same day I set about calling some numbers from the business directory (in alphabetical order, hardly missing any that could have had the slightest, even indirect connection with marketing clothes), and at the end of the day I had a blinding headache, but I was calm because I had succeeded in arranging several crucial meetings for the following day. I felt sufficiently strong to be decisive, and I had written them off, intending to cancel all but one the next morning, concentrating on the one remaining visit to the owner of an enormous commercial enterprise. When that textile king had examined Dejan's T-shirts from all sides, like Angela—with the practiced eye of an expert—and said, "They might sell," nodding his head convincingly, and then, accompanying me to the leather-lined door, tubby and comic as he was, added, "Call me by Sunday," my face lit up. Returning home in the rickety bus, I was already composing in my head the letter I would send Dejan. I believed (and now all I can do is be sickened for the rest of my life by my incurable stupidity and arrogance) that at this stage, since neither of us had a fax machine, postal communication was incomparably more elegant than discussions by telephone, and we would in any case communicate every day by telephone when things got going and came dangerously near to completion. And later, as I walked, completely oblivious of the streets that were unwinding pliantly in front of me, but led in fact by the infallible instinct of a walker, in my head I watched an optimistic filmstrip of Dejan's and my lightning path to success, illuminated by the magnificent spotlights of a Milan, Paris, or London fashion show. Not even the icy, painful rain, that shrieking paradigm of a Belgrade December, was able to sober me, nor the slippery plateau of Terazije Square, nor all the sadistic discharges of winter; I walked and walked, weaving around the sluggish bodies of other walkers, whose faces expressed the sad resignation I have already mentioned, and I smiled a smile that does not seek partnership. Strong as I was, and self-sufficient (but actually swept along by just the tail of the extraordinary power Dejan radiated, and that was spread before me now in all its force and beauty), I simply glowed. I was so carried away by my self-appointed proximity to the object of my adoration that I didn't feel like going home. I knew that would mean the end of the agreeable daydreaming I was enjoying so immensely. So I decided to go on walking, almost randomly, choosing streets following an inner guide, the logic of which, or its probable absence, did not worry me. My senses registered the outside world only intermittently, like a reliable radar system that would do nothing if a bird happened to fly across its path, but would never fail to react to an enemy aircraft. That ingrained sense of caution protected me from extreme situations: I moved without the fear that some unruly vehicle might run me over, but at the same time was so isolated that it could have happened (as it did indeed happen) that I would simply walk past a familiar person (as I did slip past Vanja, who was sitting on the high railing in Kondina Street, his feet hooked between the bars). Bustling along, I would certainly have turned the corner had he not at once jumped down after me and called, exactly as I had, once, to Dejan: "Hey!"

I turned in mid-step, as though obeying an order. Although the exclamation could have been addressed to anyone, I knew that it was meant for me. I knew, at the same instant, who it was calling me. My brain, like a devoted and adroit adjutant, pulled Vanja's face out of the register, having mechanically recorded it a second earlier and put it aside for some future use, because I was preoccupied with thoughts of Dejan and our cooperative venture. Approaching me, Vanja thrust both hands, together with something he was holding, into the pockets of his coat, which was so long that its ends dragged along the muddy asphalt. "Hi," he said, offering me his hand. His fingers stuck and clicked, like castanets. Without saying another word, just miming and smiling, he led me back to that railing and received me there, in the corner of the building, with such courteous gestures that he might have been leading me into the place where he lived (which was probably not far from the truth). With a bound, he placed himself back on the height from which he had observed me, took a handkerchief from one pocket and tied it around his forehead, and from the other a crumpled bag, which he held to his lips and began panting into rapidly, sniffing the glue. When, finally, he emerged from the bag, he seemed transformed—like Micromegas returning from an interplanetary journey. Detaching itself from the bag, his head dropped abruptly forward, and Vanja doubled over and fell headlong from the high railing so that I almost cried out in fear, but he landed neatly on his feet, in a spectacular stage fall. Once again at eye level, he hopped about a bit and then smiled. "Ooph!" he said in a satisfied tone, shaking his head. A few waxed locks of hair fell over his forehead, to meet up with his carefree smile.

I had met Vanja through Dejan. For a time we saw

each other quite regularly, but I don't remember ever having seen him in a state very different from the one described. He sang in GSG 9, but did so purely out of loyalty and love for Dejan. The other two in the group (whom I did not know, since no one knew them, and it sometimes seemed to me that the pair of them did not know each other especially well either) were subjected by Vanja, without the slightest scruple, to his public scorn. He loathed them to such an extent that there would often be a fight before a concert, and sometimes Vanja would clamber onto the stage covered in bruises, his lip cracked open, and the organizers hated them because of this tendency to scrap among themselves, and this fact limited the growth of their popularity. When I was describing GSG 9 onstage, I neglected to mention Vanja because his appearance disrupted that wonderful harmony of stereotypes, the visual harmony the other members' appearance created. Vanja truly belonged to some other world. Surrounded by Dejan, X, and Y—that trio of designer fascists, so fashionable at that time, so stylish, with their shaved heads, bare to the waist—he looked incredible in his gray Champion T-shirts, over which he wore unbuttoned checked shirts of thick flannel and jeans, also unbuttoned, which would inevitably slip down to his knees in the course of the concert, offering a view of the snake Vanja had had tattooed on his thigh a couple of years earlier in Paris. His hair represented an orthodox nest of tassels, which one could not help hoping would one day, finally, look like dreadlocks, but they remained in that miserable state, because Vanja did not want his hair to look like anything other than tassels.

"Well, I mean, I don't have a clue, fuck it," he said, wiping his nose on his sleeve, "what's up, son?" Amazed, as ever, by his private jargon, which he had developed over the years, leaving ever less space for the meaningful parts of the sentence and elaborating only a torrent of indistinct phrases, I didn't know where to start, and I informed him, briefly, that Angela had been pregnant for a full nine months but that it was beginning to look as though the child would be a day or two late. Vanja seemed to find it deeply distasteful to be supplied with this superfluous information. He didn't know what to do with it. He, who jealously guarded his local-kid image (he lived two streets from the place where we had met), rejected any thought of marriage or children with revulsion, full of an innocent, boyish mockery. Yet he was only two or three years younger than me. So as not to have to say anything, Vanja simply licked his green teeth, and mumbled, "OK, son, so, like, fuck that," and we both sank into silence—I leaning against the railing with my hands in my pockets; he, for the most part, with his head, the unhealthy color of the Belgrade dirt, in the bag. Vanja would only intermittently extract his unusual bonce in order to giggle at what was, presumably, a hallucination in the distance, or simply to take a breath of relatively fresh, but certainly unsticky, air, for a change. He used each opportunity to address passersby, and particularly girls, who gave us a wide berth. He spat often. "I'm spitting rubber bands," he told me, as though he had said "I've got something stuck in my tooth." I let him talk, and he told me, from his perch, about Ian Brady and Myra Hindley, about Charles Manson's childhood, about Goering's addiction to morphine; he also mentioned Sammy Davis, Jr., in a similar context, but I couldn't follow that. Nor could I grasp the connection between all that, all those randomly scattered facts, and an insert from the life of the serial killer Trobec, but it was stupid to look for any connection, because there most probably wasn't any. That constant leaping out of the train of his own thoughts made him resemble the Dejan of our last meeting, except that Vanja's discourse was more ragged, more aggressive, and longer. But who could have followed the demented curve of his thoughts and associations? Just when I felt he wasn't going to say anything else, and I was on the point of speaking myself, Vanja produced some little pieces of paper from somewhere and handed them to me: "Take a look, sonny," he said, and I peered at the first piece in the bundle of various clippings, but all that I could see was a black-and-white photo of Frank Sinatra, wearing a tie with a printed pattern of a panda with a blade of grass in its mouth, accompanied by Judy Garland looking like an elderly Heidi, both of them smiling professionally in front of an enormous microphone like a scarab, on which there was a plate bearing the inscription WXYZ RADIO. Then, suddenly, Vanja removed that picture from my field of vision and a different scrap of paper appeared before me. This was a clipping from an American magazine, a fragment of an interview with William Burroughs meditating on the theme of shooting as a sport. Vanja was delighted by his statement, because the whole time I was trying to decipher the text, pale from frequent handling and damp, he kept jabbing me with his elbow and giggling: "Shooting, get it?"

"You're not in the war?" I asked, taking advantage of his momentary confusion to hand him back the wad of little bits of paper, endeavoring painlessly to resist scrutinizing them further, while Vanja, shoving the clippings back into his pocket, smiled ironically. Some years previously he had invested at least half of his reason in avoiding military service, and achieved his aim, at the same time doing something for his singing (because from that time on he was able to confront the brutal music produced by GSG 9, and seize it and bite into it in his own voice), but ever since the war in Croatia began, Vanja had been doing everything in his power somehow to jump on that bandwagon. At one time he had even offered to Dejan himself to join up in his place and see what happened, but Dejan refused, not, in truth, out of pride or heroism, but out of panic-stricken fear that such a stupid machination could be easily found out, which would have made everything even more complicated for him. Of course, it was very possible that Vanja had not been completely serious either, that he had made the suggestion out of frustration, rather than genuine desire. He made three or four offers of service as a volunteer, in the course of which it emerged that he had been dealt a personalized measure of sorrow in that collective damnation, because he was rejected each time, and that was his final encounter with the Yugoslav People's Army. After that, he tried to sign up for all the existing armies on this side of the front line, but they all received him in the same way. They thanked him for his offer of assistance and demonstration of patriotism, but returned his papers without any particular explanation. "So, I think, what," he said finally, "that's like, brains, get it, brains, sonny, what, and I'm going to Croatia, why not, I can tell you that the Croatian army and the paras there pay more."

"Oh God!" I bleated, flabbergasted. I simply couldn't believe that such an announcement could be serious. But it was. It was quite clear that this was no expression of fury on Vanja's part, or complete disagreement, or bitterness, but that he was, quite simply, burning to participate in this war. For some reason that I entirely failed to comprehend, this war really appealed to Vanja. "I met up with Dejan, you know," I added, because it seemed logical to me that mention of the war should be followed by mention of our common friend who had suffered so badly in that war. But Vanja's head was already in the bag, which swelled and shrank, like a crumpled polyp that had grabbed hold of him and was actually chewing him up. The glue inside had already begun to dry up. Occupied with this activity, Vanja replied, "Uh-huh." "Yes," I went on, "and then he sent me some T-shirts he'd made, crazy, so . . . I've just been to some firms. I want to sell them for him. I feel bad about Dejan, Vanja. He's a brilliant guy, you know how Angela has always had a thing for him, and I really think he's great. His arm . . . it's really fucked up, I want to help him."

Vanja slowly took his head out of the bag and looked at me with the bloodshot eyes of an American basset hound. "T-shirts?" he said blankly.

"T-shirts, T-shirts," I replied. "Dejan's T-shirts. He's started a business. Do you see anything of him at all?"

"No," answered Vanja, with unusual vehemence. Then he hurled the bag away from him, jumped back onto the railing, and stared into the distance. "Huh, you weren't at the funeral," he said suddenly, watching a girl who happened to be walking past. Prepared for Vanja's frequent and abrupt changes of subject, his rough switching to and fro, I didn't bat an eyelid in the face of such a question.

"Whose funeral?" I responded with another question. However, Vanja sighed deeply, which was so unusual, particularly from that height where everything was clear, that I believe I had already guessed something, but insufficiently to be able to formulate it to myself. Then, his eyes quite serious, he bent toward me, intending to look into my face and see whether, from there, he could read something in it. "You don't know?" he asked, and that disconcerted me, and I didn't know how to react, apart from shrugging my shoulders. "Don't fuck around," he added. And then he did something unusual. Putting his hands together in an attitude of prayer, he acquired what could have been construed as an expression of beatitude, and then he began flapping his arms, like angel's wings. "Dejan," he said, reinforcing his pantomime, in a quiet voice.

"Dejan what? Dejan what?" I shouted, so that Vanja lurched to one side and fell off the railing again. I jumped. "Fuck you!" I shouted. "Don't do that again!" He just scratched his head. "Oh fuck," he said. "Don't hit me, please!" But then he tapped me lightly on the shoulder and came right up to me, and the overpowering stench of the glue hypnotized me. Vanja calmly kissed me on the cheek. "He killed himself, man," he whispered, as though confiding a secret.

In the Hold

I spent the rest of the day, with Angela backing me up, squabbling with her mother, who flew through our flat from room to room, on her high heels, belatedly sterilizing it, belittling our several days of labor, surprised at our negligence, weeding out dried and withered flowers, scandalized by the walls of our bathroom, which Angela, in a fit of inspiration, had stuck all over, from floor to ceiling, with little pornographic pictures. Waving her feather duster, she maintained that Angela's contractions had all but begun. That made us laugh. "I imagine I'll feel them before you do, Mother," said Angela. Vida went on enjoying the role of Mary Poppins for a while longer, but when she got tired of bustling around working, and took off her pink rubber gloves, she was overwhelmed by grief for Lazar. She wiped the tears from her cheeks with a disposable diaper, which she kissed, as though bewitched, and when she left us, she was still choking with sobs. That did it for Angela. She waddled off to bed early. Full of tenderness, I covered her up and kissed her, before turning off the light in the bedroom. In that darkness, she was so wonderfully tired that her eyes closed on their own, and she yawned one last time, smacking her lips for a while afterward, like a small child. Returning to the apple-pie living room, there was nothing left for me but to yawn at the television, talk to Pharaoh, and thank myself for having succeeded in restraining myself and sparing Angela the news of Dejan's suicide. In that atmosphere of quiet indifference to everything, I jerked off, sprawled on the sofa—out of boredom. When I joined Angela in bed, it was midnight. I think that I fell asleep (although not from a weariness that can be cured by sleep) as soon as I closed my eyes.

Vanja's announcement, and the realization of Dejan's personal *Gesamtlösung*, left me completely demoralized. I suddenly found myself in an open space that I had not anticipated, preoccupied with my commercial euphoria, and I was ashamed of that sickly humanitarian impulse which had driven me in such a pompous and insensitive way to plan a shared business life with a friend who, without my having an inkling of it in my stupidity, was on the verge of suicide. Maybe, if I had called him and said, "The T-shirts are great, we'll make a go of them," maybe, then, everything would have been different, I reflected as I made my way home on foot from Kondina Street to

Molerova, but then I was disgusted that I was attributing too much importance to my own input into the whole thing. Quite simply, Dejan had been in a situation where he had had to weigh his own chances. As an experiment, he had set out to live paranormally, to pretend that nothing had happened, but it hadn't worked. I have never claimed to be a reliable psychologist, so it isn't surprising that I misinterpreted everything. Because, evidently, Dejan was falling apart. The being I had accepted as the New Dejan obviously represented, to the stumps of Dejan's prewar, two-armed self, an ugly caricature with which he could never be reconciled. That New Being had tried to establish at least some kind of contact with its predecessor, but in the end it must have all seemed useless even to him. That being must have realized that all future efforts were superfluous. Or was this interpretation of mine mistaken? Perhaps Dejan had stopped, once and for all, in the middle of an insoluble dilemma? Perhaps he hadn't understood anything either? Perhaps he hadn't liked the T-shirts? Perhaps Jelena had offended him in some way? In any case, on my way home after my meeting with Vanja, from Kondina Street across the deserted children's playground in Tašmajdan, I resolved to keep Dejan's death to myself. I didn't feel sad, anyway, just secretly deceived, although that feeling quickly passed, and all I wanted was to burp loudly.

This tale is nearing its end, and Dejan has outstripped its framework. For, about a week later, the postman rang our doorbell one morning and handed us an enormous box, in which there were seventy-two children's T-shirts with the most various designs. This was Dejan's promised consignment of samples. In that parcel, which had taken exactly ten days to travel from one side of Belgrade to the other, there was no note, no written trace of him. Dejan had not sent me any instructions or advice. He had sent me his inheritance, for me to do with whatever I wanted.

In the transition from the murky darkness to the conditional morning, something roused me from my sleep. Angela was sitting up beside me, supporting her back with her hands the way old ladies do when they stretch. "I think it's begun," she whispered, without even looking at me, when I propped myself up on my elbows. I scratched my rough, unshaven cheek. "Oh God," I said dully, feeling awkward. "I think it's begun," Angela repeated, hoarsely this time, observing her stomach. "Well, what'll we do?" I asked, but she just rolled her eyes. "Just don't panic; there's time, let's sleep," she said.

In a synchronized movement, we returned to the horizontal. She moved closer to me, imperceptibly, and laid her head on my shoulder. I felt something warm and soft against my feet—Pharaoh had settled himself at the foot of the bed, in his usual place. A kind of psycho-twilight materialized above us; a dense, doughy mass covered us, and we felt as though we were in the hold of a ship, condemned to play the role of culprit for all the world's sufferings. Sunk in a half-sleep, Angela answered questions no one had asked, and I watched her until she began, in my eyes, to tremble like aspic. "No, no. It doesn't hurt, it doesn't hurt," she said at first. Then: "I've packed my toothbrush, maybe another bar of soap." "Mother will go into orbit . . ." "I've heard they play music." "Here it is, here it is again—not so strong . . ." she said, arranging her body as though it didn't actually belong to her. I smiled at the sleep that was doing a bad job of dividing us. It was strange, because Angela and I had never understood each other so well as at that unusual moment. I yawned and smacked my lips: "Rome, or perhaps America after all?" I asked lazily. I knew Angela would know what I meant. "Mmmmm," she replied, as though her mouth were full of a delicious cake. "Yes, yes," I affirmed in the confident, copper tone of advertisements for Japanese cars. Something swung above us, some kind of finger no doubt, like the one at the cemetery, but again—in vain. Perhaps we were in the hold, perhaps we would never get out of it, but that night it didn't matter. We laughed, both of us, heartily, but I know: we were asleep.

Appendix 1

A Compilation of Deaths: 1989, 1990, 1991

My very dear friend Petar, Angela's former boyfriend, with whom she had never (she maintained) made it to bed, was felled by sudden leukemia. I think this was the first of the string of deaths that followed. Petar was the link that joined Angela and me. We have every right to consider him the original instigator of our meeting, our relationship, our marriage, and, consequently, of our child, which was on its way. Petar was already horribly swollen, his hair was already falling out, when he traveled to Zurich for a bone marrow transplant, or something like that. That's where he died. Charlie was raped by Arabs while in detention. Charlie didn't care. In return he bequeathed them a real time bomb: the little, wartlike body of the HIV virus—he had plenty of them to spare in his body, and he passed them around unsparingly, to be honest. He died in Drajzerova Street, pale, covered in spittle, and quite beside himself. Then came the two sisters, Nina and Lea, a diplomat's children. Like characters who could easily have found their place in a potential *Lexicon of Morbid Records*, they died of the same virus as Charlie, both of them, in the short space of nine months. I remember Snotty as well. He suffered from that same problem too, and whatever I had thought about Snotty before, he proved himself the cleverest of everyone in that club. He anticipated his personal problem: he treated himself to an overdose. One cold evening, Divna somehow staggered home. Spaced-out and exhausted, she fell asleep on the toilet, a deep, heroin-induced sleep, with her panties around her ankles. Her head fell awkwardly backward, and when her father found her the next morning, in that same position, she was already white and cold. She had choked on her own tongue. Olga's left breast started to excrete something white and cheesy, which couldn't be stopped. She liked to swear like a trooper, usually in the most awkward places, and I can imagine what she did to the doctors, but they just clucked helplessly over her, until the last day. We all hated Danny's girl, Jasna. Danny was so soft, we felt that she was just playing with his weakness. Although each of us on his own account had tried to convince him that Jasna was trash, Danny smiled as though he didn't believe us. One day he stood up, stretched, and jumped out the window. I know this because his mother told me: she had been in the same room. His girl, Jasna, that bitch, staggered us all when, just a couple of days after Danny's suicide, she was found hanging from a beam in her parents' house.

Appendix 2

Chronicle of the Escapees: 1990, 1991

Once we used to meet up every day with Sile and Lana. In the spring of 1991 they went off to Utrecht. They had both qualified as doctors here, and now she is working as a baby-sitter in two different places and cleaning a flat on the weekend; he found a job after several months of fruitless searching—an Indian in a restaurant in their neighbor-hood took him on as an assistant. Vera is in London, before that she was in Hawaii, but I don't know much about her, because we aren't in touch. Once I met her brother, Jovan: he told me that he was preparing to beat it to Amsterdam, unless they picked him up first, since the drafters had already come to his door several times. Sasa was sharing an East London studio with a girlfriend from Istanbul, he lived on fish and chips, and stared at red brick buildings. Sometimes a raindrop would hit him in the eye. He had no money, he was sort of starving, the landlord had threatened to throw him and the Turkish girl, who was fat and noisy, out of the flat if they did not pay all the rent they owed by the end of the week. Otherwise, he was fine. He had found a broken phone box from which he telephoned Belgrade for two whole months without paying anything. That was why I knew more about him than the others. Uros was working as a steward. Now he was in Singapore with a wife and two cats. No one knew anything about him. Angela maintains that in Singapore people eat cats the way we eat chicken—perhaps they had taken them with them to sell, if worse came to worst? What drove Lola to put her foot up on a polished wall in the middle of Madrid and sell herself to the first comer, just like that, blond, bright, and noble, for a heap of pesetas? Just before Christmas 1991, Nenad finally set off in a new Suzuki from Washington to Seattle to meet up with his lover by correspondence, a sixty-four-year-old psychiatrist. As he entered the great city, he squinted at the enormous advertisements on both sides of the freeway. . . .

But I'm just mentioning all of them in passing. What I really want to do is write about Darko, because I have a kind of ambivalent feeling about him. Darko was my schoolmate, one of many, and nothing more than that. One beside the other, in little red synthetic pants, we made a caterpillar at a jamboree in honor of President Tito's birthday. In the midst of the crammed, excited stadium, his palms were wet, as always. He put the wrong foot forward and broke away from me, and the whole caterpillar nearly stumbled as a result of his stupidity. Some boys began to giggle. Beads of sweat appeared on our gymnastics teacher's forehead. However, the good-humored auditorium, the functionaries in their broad ties and Tito in his ceremonial box, thought it was sweet. We were rewarded with spontaneous applause, and later everyone said it had been the best rally ever. Darko's mark for behavior, lowered earlier for some reason, was discreetly put right. I didn't like that Darko at all—perhaps that's why I'm writing so much about him? I found him too fat, he wore stale-smelling clothes, he would gouge out a quarter loaf and fill it with chips, I was horrified by his habit of catching lizards and cutting off their tails, he always dragged an old Vicks inhaler around in the pocket of his threadbare coat. He had needed only a few years of mutual nonmeeting for him to be transformed into an academic ascetic—a kind of distant relation of Lazar's. To be more precise, this consumer of cheap sausages had become a vegetarian and was touchingly disgusted by smoking. He edited a young people's literary magazine, he had met Czesław Milosz, Kundera, and the like. Everything was in front of him, but suddenly he disappeared. He went to Sweden and married his Swedish girlfriend of several years' standing, of whose existence no one had known anything up until then, and it remained a mystery how Darko, who had spent the greatest part of his life in Belgrade, had been able to maintain that relationship at all. In any case, he was happily married. They moved out of her parents' house within reach of Stockholm into the city. They have a three-and-a-half-room flat looking out onto an orderly park. She received an allowance from her father; he was well paid as an editor at a radio station for our refugees. One of the few who got his bearings, but that's what he was like. Some simply, always and everywhere, manage, life stretches before them like an endless red carpet. Perhaps that's why I didn't like him, and it's certainly why I'm writing about him. He was just a schoolmate, nothing important, and now I feel I would like to spend time with him. I no longer know how to conjure up the stench of his school jacket; sometimes I think: Perhaps he never existed. Of everything I ever knew about Darko, all that was left was an ephemeral attractiveness. I felt like writing him a letter. I would dedicate a poem to him. I'm not at all sure that I had interpreted him correctly. Perhaps, with a little more effort, now when there hardly exists the possibility of such a thing, we would succeed in proving that we were made to be friends, hand in glove.

A NOTE ABOUT THE AUTHOR

Vladimir Arsenijević was born in Pula, Yugoslavia, in 1965. In 1995 he became the youngest recipient ever of the NIN Prize, his country's most prestigious literary honor. This is his first novel. He lives and works in Belgrade.

A NOTE ON THE TYPE

The text of this book has been set in a typeface called Poliphilus. This face is a copy of a roman type that Francesco Griffo cut for the Venetian printer Aldus Manutius in 1499.

The italic of Poliphilus is called Blado. It is named after the Roman printer Antonio Blado, who printed many books in this font, using it as an individual type and not as a subsidiary to the roman.

Composed by PennSet, Inc., Bloomsburg, Pennsylvania
Printed and bound by The Haddon Craftsmen, Scranton, Pennsylvania
Designed by Robert C. Olsson